Withdrawn

MORRIGHAN

THE BEGINNINGS OF THE
REMNANT UNIVERSE

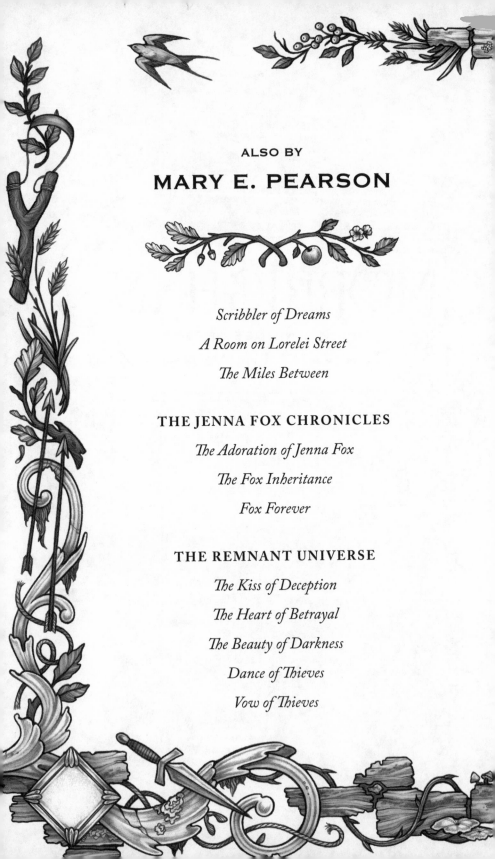

ALSO BY

MARY E. PEARSON

Scribbler of Dreams

A Room on Lorelei Street

The Miles Between

THE JENNA FOX CHRONICLES

The Adoration of Jenna Fox

The Fox Inheritance

Fox Forever

THE REMNANT UNIVERSE

The Kiss of Deception

The Heart of Betrayal

The Beauty of Darkness

Dance of Thieves

Vow of Thieves

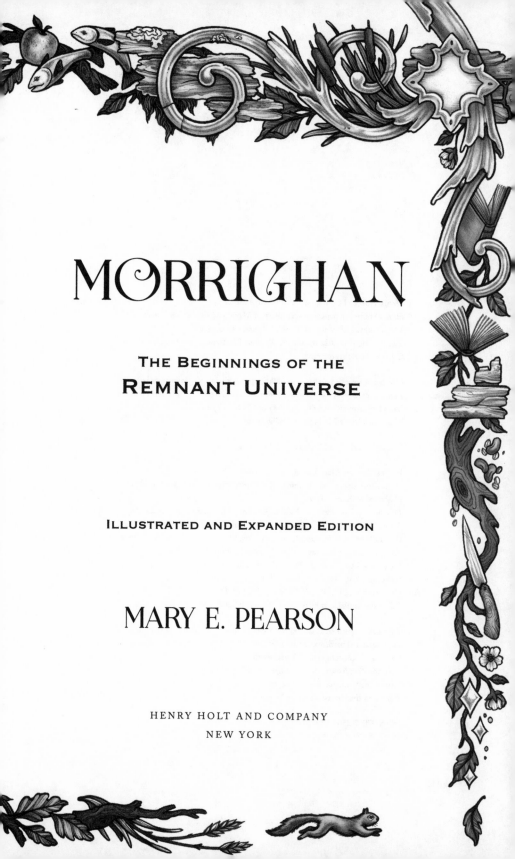

MORRIGHAN

THE BEGINNINGS OF THE
REMNANT UNIVERSE

ILLUSTRATED AND EXPANDED EDITION

MARY E. PEARSON

HENRY HOLT AND COMPANY
NEW YORK

Henry Holt and Company, *Publishers since 1866*
Henry Holt® is a registered trademark of Macmillan Publishing Group, LLC
120 Broadway, New York, NY 10271 • fiercereads.com
Text copyright © 2022 by Mary E. Pearson. Illustrations copyright © 2022 by Kate
O'Hara. All rights reserved.

Our books may be purchased in bulk for promotional, educational, or business use.
Please contact your local bookseller or the Macmillan Corporate and Premium
Sales Department at (800) 221-7945 ext. 5442 or by email at
MacmillanSpecialMarkets@macmillan.com.

Library of Congress Cataloging-in-Publication Data

Names: Pearson, Mary E., author. | O'Hara, Kate, illustrator.
Title: Morrighan : the beginnings of the Remnant universe / Mary E. Pearson;
illustrated by Kate O'Hara.
Description: First edition. | New York : Henry Holt and Company, 2022. |
Series: The Remnant chronicles ; book 4. | Audience: Ages 14-18. | Audience:
Grades 10-12. | Summary: Against all odds, Morrighan and Jafir, members of
opposing tribes, fall in love and set history in motion.
Identifiers: LCCN 2022017598 | ISBN 9781250868350 (hardcover)
Subjects: CYAC: Fantasy. | LCGFT: Fantasy fiction. | Novellas.
Classification: LCC PZ7.P32316 Mo 2022 | DDC [Fic]—dc23
LC record available at https://lccn.loc.gov/2022017598

Originally published as an ebook novella in January 2016 by Henry Holt and Company
First expanded hardcover edition, 2022
Original ebook designed by Anna Booth
Expanded hardcover edition designed by Mallory Grigg
Artist's medium: ink on paper, digital
Printed in the United States of America

ISBN 978-1-250-86835-0
10 9 8 7 6 5 4 3 2 1

For Ava, Emily, Leah, and Riley,
and the journeys yet to come

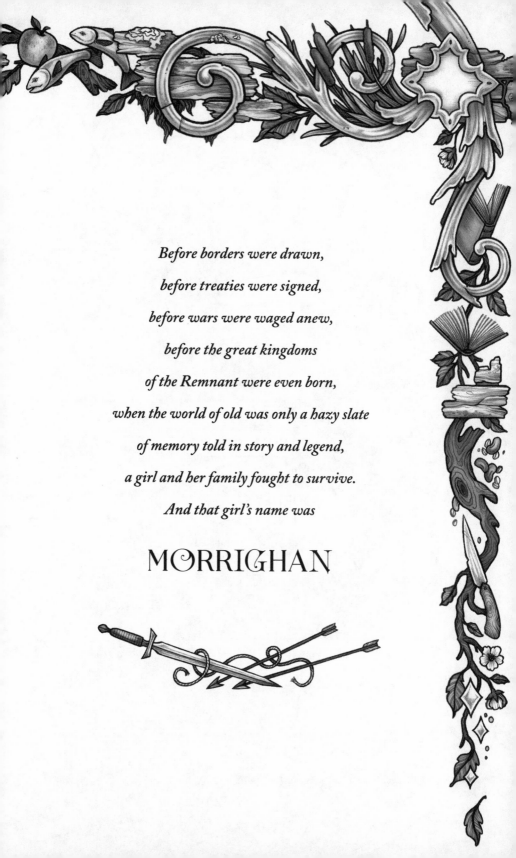

Before borders were drawn,

before treaties were signed,

before wars were waged anew,

before the great kingdoms

of the Remnant were even born,

when the world of old was only a hazy slate

of memory told in story and legend,

a girl and her family fought to survive.

And that girl's name was

MORRIGHAN

TOR'S WATCH

VALLEY OF RUINS

X JOURNEY'S
END

She asks for another story,

one to pass the time and fill her.

I search for the truth, the details of a world so long

past now, I'm not sure it ever was.

Once upon a time, so very long ago,
In an age before monsters and demons roamed the earth,
A time when children ran free in meadows,
And heavy fruit hung from trees,
There were cities, large and beautiful,
with sparkling towers that touched the sky.

—Were they made of magic?

I was only a child myself. I thought they could hold a

whole world. To me they were made of—

Yes, they were spun of magic
and light and the dreams of gods.

—And there was a princess?

I smile.

Yes, my child, a precious princess just like you.
She had a garden filled with trees
that hung with fruit as big as a man's fist.

The child looks at me, doubtful.

She has never seen an apple, but she has seen the fists of men.

—Are there really such gardens, Ama?

Not anymore.

Yes, my child, somewhere. And one day you will find them.

—THE LAST TESTAMENTS OF GAUDREL

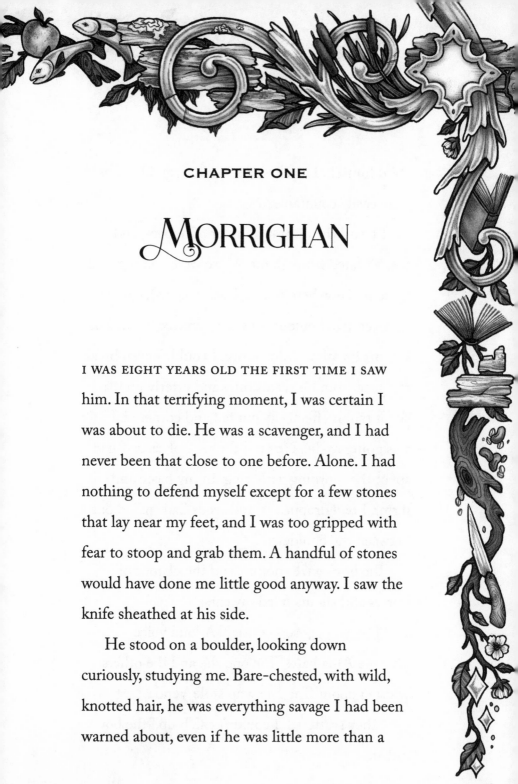

CHAPTER ONE

Morrighan

I WAS EIGHT YEARS OLD THE FIRST TIME I SAW him. In that terrifying moment, I was certain I was about to die. He was a scavenger, and I had never been that close to one before. Alone. I had nothing to defend myself except for a few stones that lay near my feet, and I was too gripped with fear to stoop and grab them. A handful of stones would have done me little good anyway. I saw the knife sheathed at his side.

He stood on a boulder, looking down curiously, studying me. Bare-chested, with wild, knotted hair, he was everything savage I had been warned about, even if he was little more than a

child himself. His chest was narrow, and his ribs were easily countable.

I heard the distant thunder of hooves, and fear vibrated through me. More were coming, and there was nowhere to run. I was trapped, cowering between two boulders in a dark crevice below him. I didn't breathe. Didn't move. I couldn't even break my gaze from his. I was fully and utterly prey, a silent rabbit effectively hunted and cornered. I was going to die. He eyed the sack of seeds I had spent the morning gathering. In my haste and terror, I had dropped it, and seeds had spilled out between the boulders.

The boy's gaze shot up, and the clamor of horses and shouts filled my ears.

"Did you get something?" A loud voice. The one Ama hates. The one she and the others whisper about. The one who stole Venda.

"They scattered. I couldn't catch up," the boy called.

Another disgusted voice. "And nothing was left behind?"

The boy shook his head.

There were more shouts of discontent and then the rumble of hooves again. Leaving. They were leaving. The boy climbed down from the boulder and left too, without another glance or word to me, his face deliberately turned away, almost as if he were shamed.

I didn't see him for another two years. The close call had instilled a heavy dose of fear in me, and I didn't wander far from the tribe again. At least, not until one warm spring day. The scavengers had seemed to move on. We'd seen no sign of them since the first frost of autumn.

But there he was, a head taller and trying to

pull cattails from my favorite pond. His blond
hair had only grown wilder, his shoulders slightly
wider, his ribs as evident as ever. I watched his
frustration swell as the stalks he pulled broke
off one after another and he came up with only
worthless pieces of stems.

"You're impatient."

He spun, drawing his knife.

Even at the tender age of ten, I knew I was
taking a risk exposing myself. I wasn't even sure

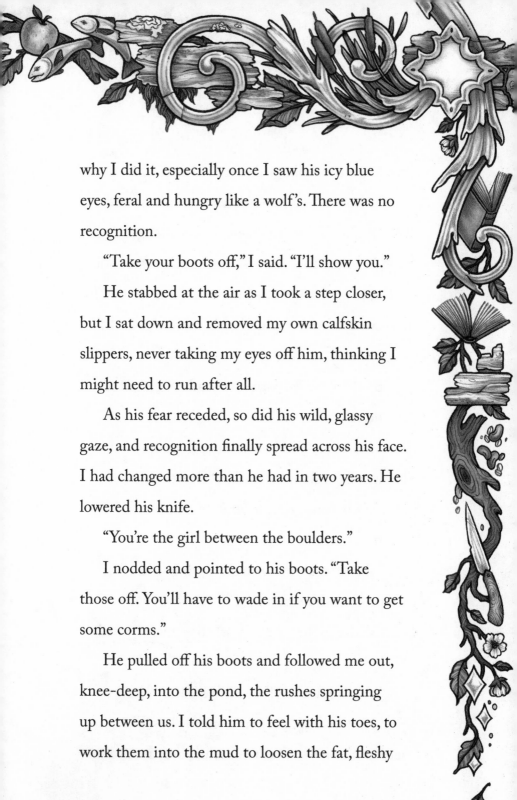

why I did it, especially once I saw his icy blue eyes, feral and hungry like a wolf's. There was no recognition.

"Take your boots off," I said. "I'll show you."

He stabbed at the air as I took a step closer, but I sat down and removed my own calfskin slippers, never taking my eyes off him, thinking I might need to run after all.

As his fear receded, so did his wild, glassy gaze, and recognition finally spread across his face. I had changed more than he had in two years. He lowered his knife.

"You're the girl between the boulders."

I nodded and pointed to his boots. "Take those off. You'll have to wade in if you want to get some corms."

He pulled off his boots and followed me out, knee-deep, into the pond, the rushes springing up between us. I told him to feel with his toes, to work them into the mud to loosen the fat, fleshy

tubers before pulling. Our toes had to do as much of the work as our hands. There were few words between us. What was there for a scavenger and a child of the Remnant to say to each other? All we had in common was hunger. But he seemed to understand I was paying him back for his act of mercy two years ago.

By the time we parted, he had a sack full of the fleshy roots.

"This is my pond now," he said sharply as he tied the sack to his saddle. "Don't come here again." He spit on the ground to emphasize his point.

I knew what he was really saying. The others would come here now too. It wouldn't be safe.

"What's your name?" I asked as he mounted his horse.

"You are nothing!" he answered, as if he'd heard a different question from my lips. He settled into his saddle, then reluctantly looked my

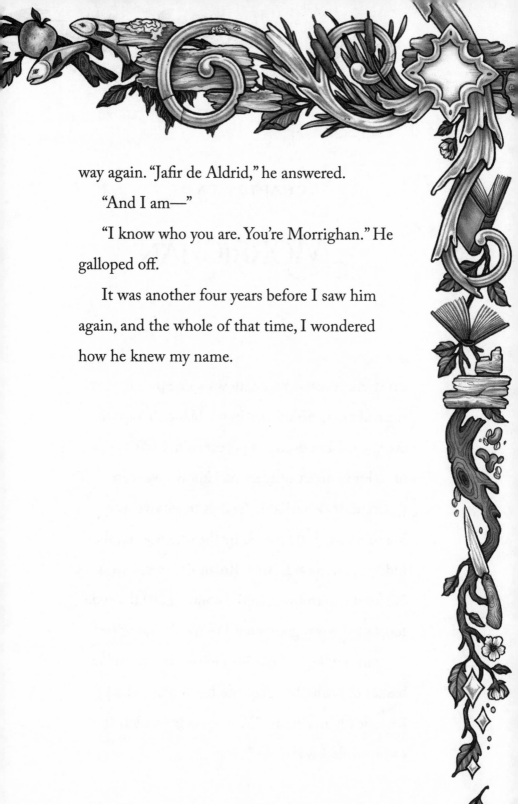

way again. "Jafir de Aldrid," he answered.

"And I am—"

"I know who you are. You're Morrighan." He galloped off.

It was another four years before I saw him again, and the whole of that time, I wondered how he knew my name.

CHAPTER TWO

MORRIGHAN

I HAD RETURNED TO CAMP WARILY THAT DAY. IT seemed being afraid was in my blood. It kept me ever aware, but even at ten years old, I was weary of it. From an early age, I had known we were different. It was what helped us to survive. But it also meant little passed by the others, even the hidden and unsaid. Ama, Rhiann, Carys, Oni, and Nedra were strongest in the knowing. And Venda too, but she was gone now. We didn't talk of her.

Ama spoke without lifting her gaze from her basket of beans, her gray and black hair pulled back neatly in a braid. "Pata tells me you left the camp while I was gone."

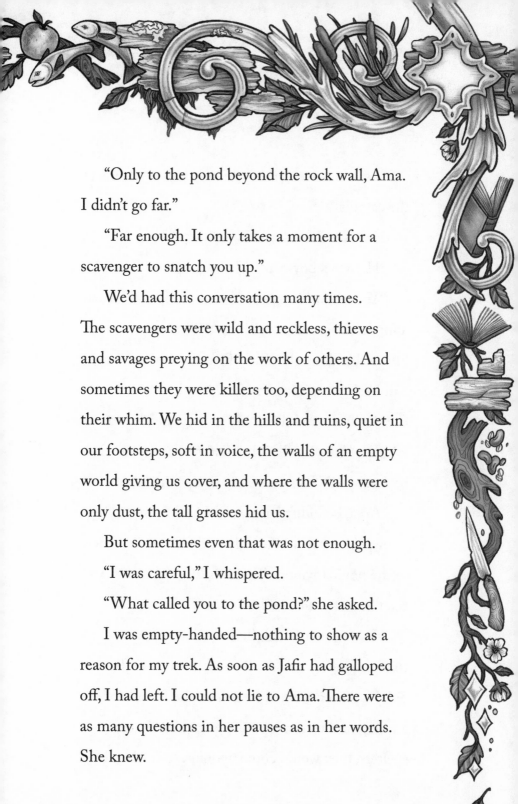

"Only to the pond beyond the rock wall, Ama. I didn't go far."

"Far enough. It only takes a moment for a scavenger to snatch you up."

We'd had this conversation many times. The scavengers were wild and reckless, thieves and savages preying on the work of others. And sometimes they were killers too, depending on their whim. We hid in the hills and ruins, quiet in our footsteps, soft in voice, the walls of an empty world giving us cover, and where the walls were only dust, the tall grasses hid us.

But sometimes even that was not enough.

"I was careful," I whispered.

"What called you to the pond?" she asked.

I was empty-handed—nothing to show as a reason for my trek. As soon as Jafir had galloped off, I had left. I could not lie to Ama. There were as many questions in her pauses as in her words. She knew.

"I saw a scavenger boy there. He was tearing at the cattails."

Her eyes darted up. "You didn't—"

"He was a boy named Jafir."

"You know his name? You *spoke* to him?" Ama jumped to her feet, scattering the beans in her lap. She grabbed my shoulders first, then brushed my hair back, examining my face. Her hands traveled frantically up and down my arms, searching for injuries. "Are you all right? Did he harm you? Did he *touch* you?" Her eyes were sharp with fear.

"Ama, he didn't harm me," I said firmly, trying to dispel her fears. "He only told me not to come to the pond anymore. That it is his pond now. And then he left with a sack of corms."

Her face hardened. I knew what she was thinking—*They take it all*—and it was true. They did. Just when we had settled on the far side of a valley, or meadow, or among the abandoned shelters, they would come upon us, to steal and

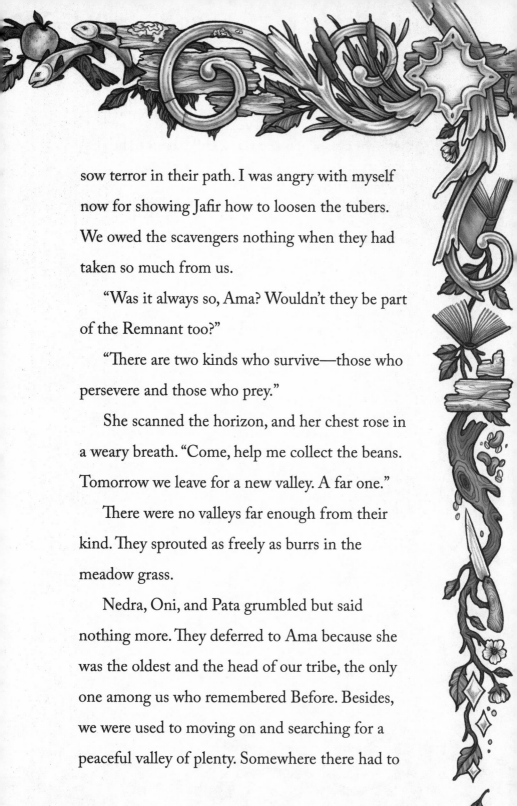

sow terror in their path. I was angry with myself now for showing Jafir how to loosen the tubers. We owed the scavengers nothing when they had taken so much from us.

"Was it always so, Ama? Wouldn't they be part of the Remnant too?"

"There are two kinds who survive—those who persevere and those who prey."

She scanned the horizon, and her chest rose in a weary breath. "Come, help me collect the beans. Tomorrow we leave for a new valley. A far one."

There were no valleys far enough from their kind. They sprouted as freely as burrs in the meadow grass.

Nedra, Oni, and Pata grumbled but said nothing more. They deferred to Ama because she was the oldest and the head of our tribe, the only one among us who remembered Before. Besides, we were used to moving on and searching for a peaceful valley of plenty. Somewhere there had to

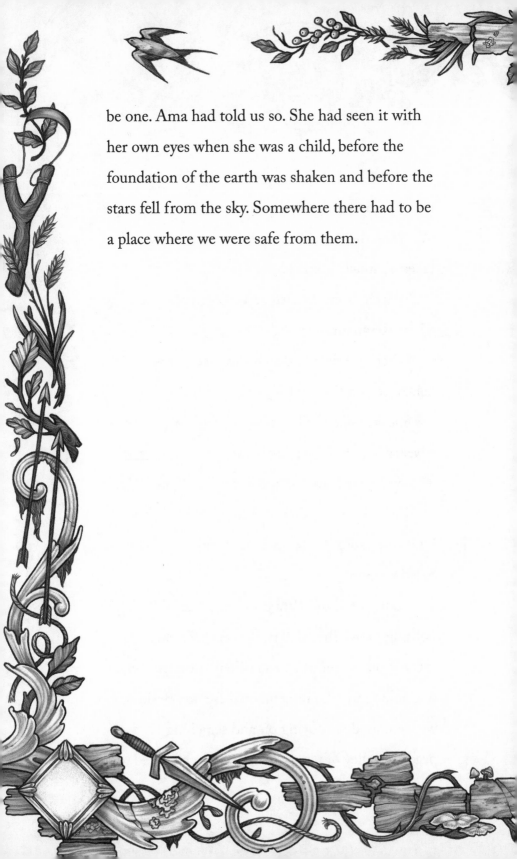

be one. Ama had told us so. She had seen it with her own eyes when she was a child, before the foundation of the earth was shaken and before the stars fell from the sky. Somewhere there had to be a place where we were safe from them.

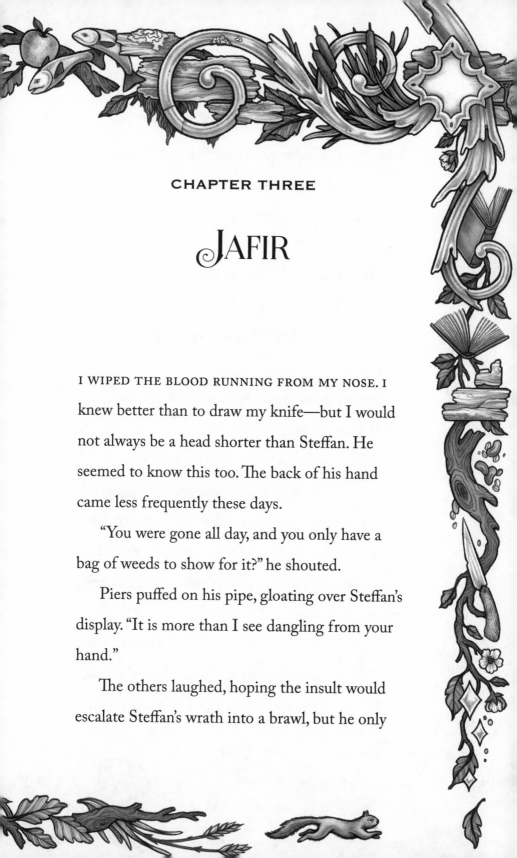

CHAPTER THREE

JAFIR

I WIPED THE BLOOD RUNNING FROM MY NOSE. I knew better than to draw my knife—but I would not always be a head shorter than Steffan. He seemed to know this too. The back of his hand came less frequently these days.

"You were gone all day, and you only have a bag of weeds to show for it?" he shouted.

Piers puffed on his pipe, gloating over Steffan's display. "It is more than I see dangling from your hand."

The others laughed, hoping the insult would escalate Steffan's wrath into a brawl, but he only waved away Piers's remark with disgust. "I can't bring home a suckling pig every day. We must all contribute things of worth."

"You stole the pig. Five minutes of effort," Piers countered.

"What is your point, old man? It filled your stomach, didn't it?"

Liam snorted. "It didn't fill mine. You should have stolen two."

Fergus threw a rock, telling them all to shut up. He was hungry.

So it went every night, our camp always on the edge of hot words and fists, but our strength came from one another too. We *were* strong. No one crossed us for fear of consequence. We had horses. We had weapons. We had earned the right to cut others down.

Laurida waved me over, and I dumped out my bag. We both began cutting off the tender corms, then peeling the tougher stalks. I had known she would be pleased. She favored the green shoots, frying them up in pig fat, and ground the larger stalks into flour. Bread was a rarity for us—unless it was stolen too.

"Where did you find them?" Laurida asked.

I looked at her, startled. "Find what?"

"These," she said, holding up a handful of the cut stalks. "What's the matter with you? Did the sun fry your brain?"

The stalks. Of course. That was all she meant. "A pond. What difference does it make?" I snapped back.

She hit me on the side of the head, then leaned closer, examining my bloodied nose. "He'll break it one of these days," she growled. "For the better. You're too pretty anyway."

The pond was already forgotten. I could not tell them that the girl had found me at the pond today, stalked me, fallen upon me without warning, rather than the other way around. I

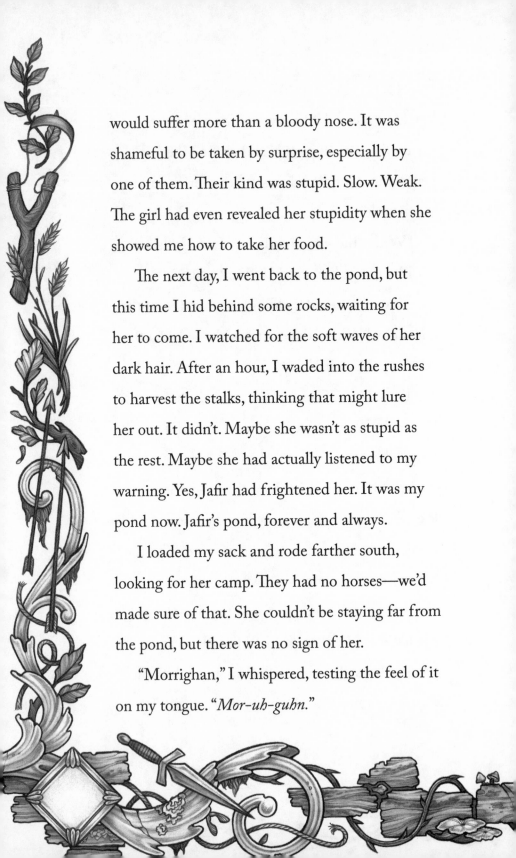

would suffer more than a bloody nose. It was shameful to be taken by surprise, especially by one of them. Their kind was stupid. Slow. Weak. The girl had even revealed her stupidity when she showed me how to take her food.

The next day, I went back to the pond, but this time I hid behind some rocks, waiting for her to come. I watched for the soft waves of her dark hair. After an hour, I waded into the rushes to harvest the stalks, thinking that might lure her out. It didn't. Maybe she wasn't as stupid as the rest. Maybe she had actually listened to my warning. Yes, Jafir had frightened her. It was my pond now. Jafir's pond, forever and always.

I loaded my sack and rode farther south, looking for her camp. They had no horses—we'd made sure of that. She couldn't be staying far from the pond, but there was no sign of her.

"Morrighan," I whispered, testing the feel of it on my tongue. "*Mor-uh-guhn.*"

Harik didn't even know my name. He called me something different each time he visited. But he knew hers. Why would the greatest warrior of the land know the name of a thin, weak girl? Especially one of them.

When I found her, I would make her tell me. And then I would hold my knife to her throat until she cried and begged for me to let her go. Just like Fergus and Steffan did with the tribespeople who hid food from us.

From a hilltop, I looked across the valleys, empty except for the wind waving a few grasses.

The girl hid well. I did not find her again for four more years.

CHAPTER FOUR

MORRIGHAN

"HERE," PATA SAID. "THIS IS A GOOD PLACE."

A twisted path had brought us there, one not easily followed, a path that I had helped find, the knowing taking root in me and growing stronger.

Ama eyed the thicket of trees. She eyed the leaning and fallen ruins for potential shelters. She eyed the hills and stony bluffs that hid us from view. But mostly I saw her eyeing the tribe. They were tired. They were hungry. They mourned. Rhiann had died at the hands of a scavenger when she refused to let go of a baby goat in her arms.

Ama looked back at the small vale and nodded. I could hear the tribe's heartbeat as well

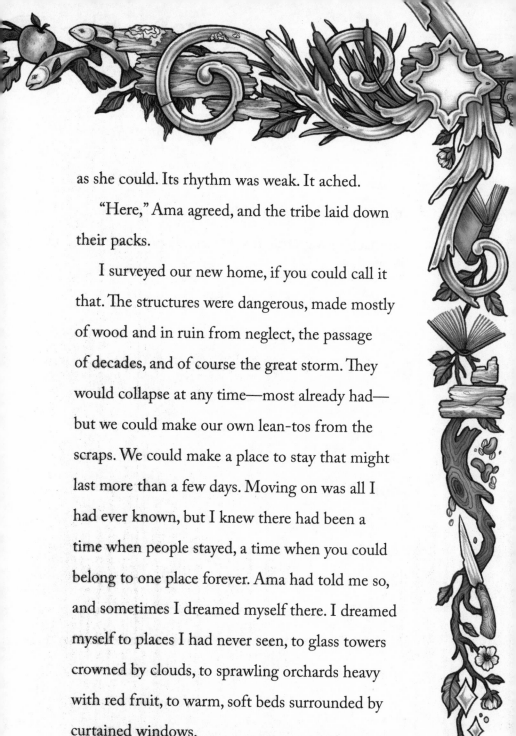

as she could. Its rhythm was weak. It ached.

"Here," Ama agreed, and the tribe laid down their packs.

I surveyed our new home, if you could call it that. The structures were dangerous, made mostly of wood and in ruin from neglect, the passage of decades, and of course the great storm. They would collapse at any time—most already had—but we could make our own lean-tos from the scraps. We could make a place to stay that might last more than a few days. Moving on was all I had ever known, but I knew there had been a time when people stayed, a time when you could belong to one place forever. Ama had told me so, and sometimes I dreamed myself there. I dreamed myself to places I had never seen, to glass towers crowned by clouds, to sprawling orchards heavy with red fruit, to warm, soft beds surrounded by curtained windows.

These were the places that Ama described

in her stories, places where all the children of the tribe were princes and princesses and their stomachs always full. It was a once-upon-a-time world that used to be.

In the last month since Rhiann's death, we had never stayed anywhere for more than a day or two. Bands of scavengers had run us off after taking our food. The encounter with Rhiann had been the worst. We'd been walking for weeks, gathering little along the way. The south had proved no safer than the north, and to the east, Harik ruled, his reach and reign growing every day. To the west over the mountains, the sickness of the storm still lingered, and beyond that, wild creatures roamed freely. Like us, they were hungry and preyed on anyone foolish enough to range there. At least, that is what I was told—no one I knew had crossed the barren mountains. We were hemmed in on all sides, always looking for a small hidden corner to settle. At least we had one another. We

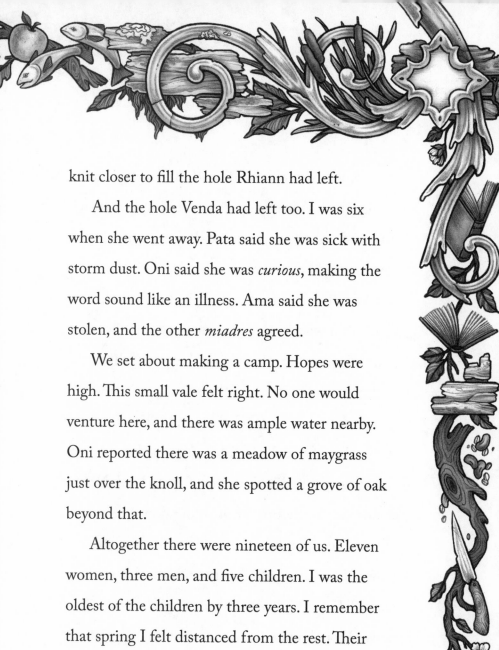

knit closer to fill the hole Rhiann had left.

And the hole Venda had left too. I was six when she went away. Pata said she was sick with storm dust. Oni said she was *curious*, making the word sound like an illness. Ama said she was stolen, and the other *miadres* agreed.

We set about making a camp. Hopes were high. This small vale felt right. No one would venture here, and there was ample water nearby. Oni reported there was a meadow of maygrass just over the knoll, and she spotted a grove of oak beyond that.

Altogether there were nineteen of us. Eleven women, three men, and five children. I was the oldest of the children by three years. I remember that spring I felt distanced from the rest. Their play annoyed me. I knew I was on the brink of something different, but with all the sameness of our daily lives, I couldn't imagine what that something might be. Every day was like the one

before. We survived. We feared. And sometimes
we laughed. What was the new feeling that stirred
in me? I wasn't sure I liked it. It was a rumbling
something like hunger.

We all helped to drag the pieces of wood,
some of it with large letters that had once been
part of something else, a partial message that
didn't matter anymore. Others found rusty metal
sheets to lean against piled rocks. I grabbed a
large plank flecked with blue. Ama said the world
was once painted with colors of every kind. Now
blue was a rarity, usually only found in the sky
or in a clear pond that reflected it, like the pond
where I had seen Jafir. Four winters had passed
since I'd seen him last. I wondered if he was still
alive. Though our tribe was ever on the edge of
starvation, the scavengers were on the edge of
something worse. They didn't care for their own
the way we did.

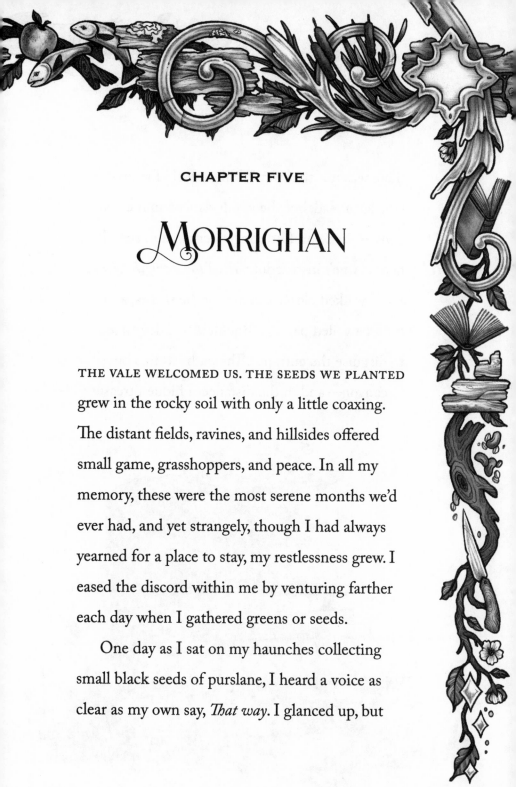

CHAPTER FIVE

MORRIGHAN

THE VALE WELCOMED US. THE SEEDS WE PLANTED
grew in the rocky soil with only a little coaxing.
The distant fields, ravines, and hillsides offered
small game, grasshoppers, and peace. In all my
memory, these were the most serene months we'd
ever had, and yet strangely, though I had always
yearned for a place to stay, my restlessness grew. I
eased the discord within me by venturing farther
each day when I gathered greens or seeds.

One day as I sat on my haunches collecting
small black seeds of purslane, I heard a voice as
clear as my own say, *That way.* I glanced up, but

there was no "that way." Only a wall of stone and vine lay ahead, but the words danced in me, *that way*, excited and fluttering—certain and sure. I heard Ama's instruction: *Trust the strength within you.* I walked closer, examining the stones, and found a veiled passage. Boulders blended together to disguise the entrance. The path led to a boxed-in canyon—and in the distance, a hidden treasure

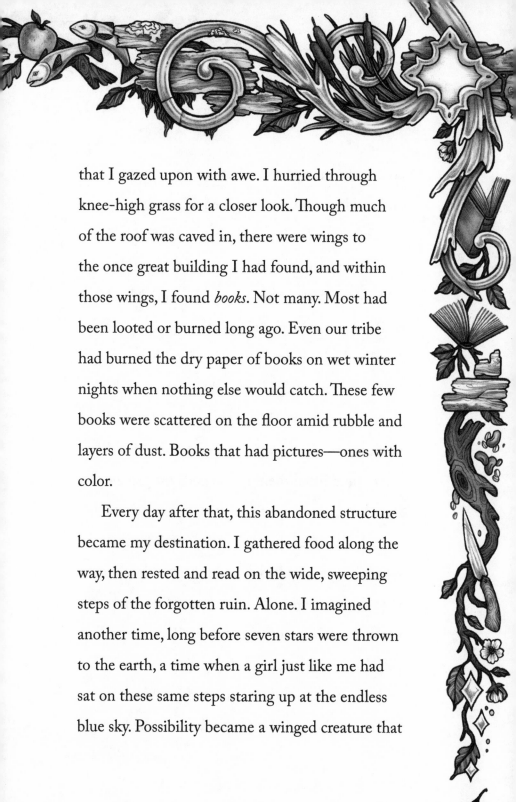

that I gazed upon with awe. I hurried through
knee-high grass for a closer look. Though much
of the roof was caved in, there were wings to
the once great building I had found, and within
those wings, I found *books*. Not many. Most had
been looted or burned long ago. Even our tribe
had burned the dry paper of books on wet winter
nights when nothing else would catch. These few
books were scattered on the floor amid rubble and
layers of dust. Books that had pictures—ones with
color.

Every day after that, this abandoned structure
became my destination. I gathered food along the
way, then rested and read on the wide, sweeping
steps of the forgotten ruin. Alone. I imagined
another time, long before seven stars were thrown
to the earth, a time when a girl just like me had
sat on these same steps staring up at the endless
blue sky. Possibility became a winged creature that

could take me anywhere I asked. I was wanton and reckless with my imagined wanderings.

Day after day, it was the same. Until one day.

I saw him out of the corner of my eye. At first I was startled, then angry, thinking Micah or Brynna had tagged along after me, but then I realized who it was. His wild blond hair was still the same, except longer than before, and it shone between the thick shrubs like a rare stalk of golden corn. *Crazy fool*, I thought, then kissed my fingers and lifted them to the gods for penance. Ama wasn't sure exactly how many gods there were. Sometimes she said one, sometimes three or four—her parents hadn't had time to school her in such things—but however many there were, I knew it was best not to test them. They controlled the stars of heaven, guided the winds of earth, and numbered our days here in the wilderness, and somewhere in Ama's recollection, she knew

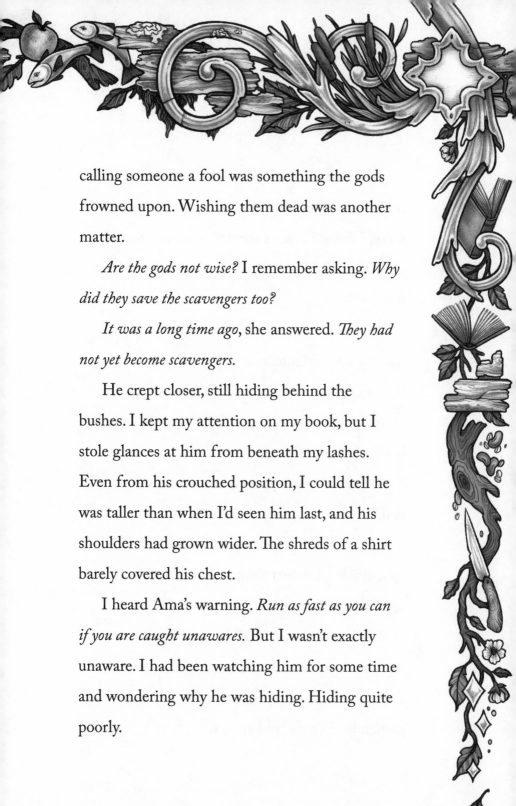

calling someone a fool was something the gods frowned upon. Wishing them dead was another matter.

Are the gods not wise? I remember asking. *Why did they save the scavengers too?*

It was a long time ago, she answered. *They had not yet become scavengers.*

He crept closer, still hiding behind the bushes. I kept my attention on my book, but I stole glances at him from beneath my lashes. Even from his crouched position, I could tell he was taller than when I'd seen him last, and his shoulders had grown wider. The shreds of a shirt barely covered his chest.

I heard Ama's warning. *Run as fast as you can if you are caught unawares.* But I wasn't exactly unaware. I had been watching him for some time and wondering why he was hiding. Hiding quite poorly.

I knew it was coming, so when he burst
from the bushes, shouting and brandishing his
knife, I didn't blink or startle but slowly turned
the page I had finished, settling in with the next
one.

"What's the matter with you?" he yelled.
"Are you not frightened?"

I raised my gaze to his. "Of what? I think it
is you who is frightened, hiding in the bushes
for the better part of an hour."

"Maybe I was planning how I would kill
you."

"If you were going to kill me, you would
have done it the first time we met. Or the
second time. Or—"

"What are you doing?" he asked, eyeing my
book and standing on the steps like he owned
them. He was just like all the other scavengers—
demanding, crude, and smelly.

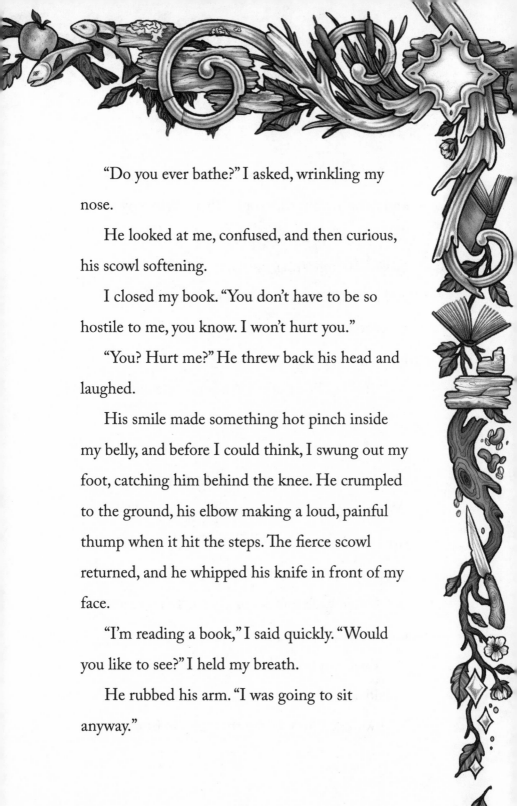

"Do you ever bathe?" I asked, wrinkling my nose.

He looked at me, confused, and then curious, his scowl softening.

I closed my book. "You don't have to be so hostile to me, you know. I won't hurt you."

"You? Hurt me?" He threw back his head and laughed.

His smile made something hot pinch inside my belly, and before I could think, I swung out my foot, catching him behind the knee. He crumpled to the ground, his elbow making a loud, painful thump when it hit the steps. The fierce scowl returned, and he whipped his knife in front of my face.

"I'm reading a book," I said quickly. "Would you like to see?" I held my breath.

He rubbed his arm. "I was going to sit anyway."

I showed him the book, turning the pages and pointing out the words. There were only a few on each page. *Moon. Night. Stars.* He was fascinated, repeating the words as I said them, and he set his knife down beside him. He touched the colorful pages rippled with time, his fingertips barely skimming them.

"This is a book of the Ancients," he said.

"Ancients? Is that what your kind call them?"

He looked at me uncertainly, then stood. "Why do you question everything I say?" He stormed down the steps, and strangely, I was sad to see him go.

"Come back tomorrow," I called. "I'll read more to you."

"I will not be back!" he yelled over his shoulder.

I watched him stomp through the brush,

only his wild blond hair shimmering above the weeds until both he and his grumbling threats disappeared.

Yes, Jafir, I thought, *you will be back, though I'm not sure why.*

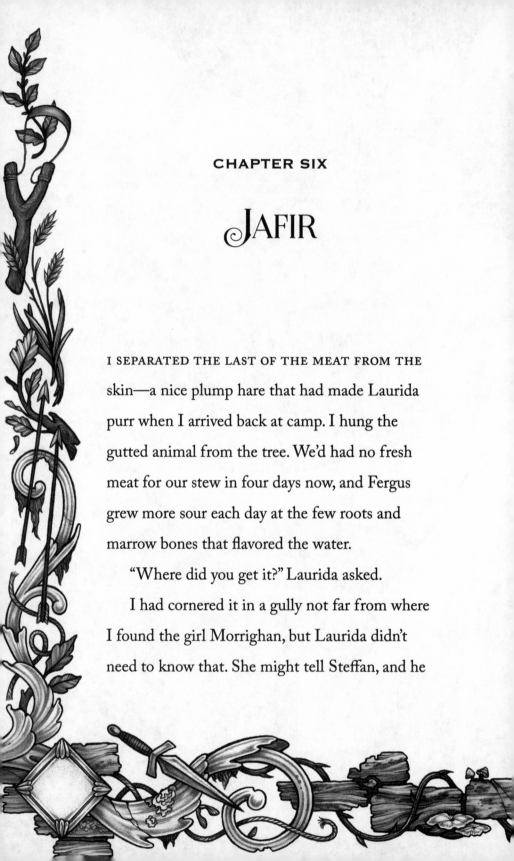

CHAPTER SIX

JAFIR

I SEPARATED THE LAST OF THE MEAT FROM THE skin—a nice plump hare that had made Laurida purr when I arrived back at camp. I hung the gutted animal from the tree. We'd had no fresh meat for our stew in four days now, and Fergus grew more sour each day at the few roots and marrow bones that flavored the water.

"Where did you get it?" Laurida asked.

I had cornered it in a gully not far from where I found the girl Morrighan, but Laurida didn't need to know that. She might tell Steffan, and he would take over my hunting ground like he took over everything else.

"In the basin past the mudflats," I answered.

"Hmm," she said suspiciously.

"I didn't steal it," I added. "I hunted it." Though in the end, it made no difference—food was food—Laurida seemed to enjoy the hunted kind more. "I'll go rinse these." I grabbed the intestines to wash in the creek.

"Walk wide around Steffan this day," she called after me. "He's in a surly temper."

I shrugged as I walked away. When was Steffan *not* in a surly temper? At least tonight he couldn't box my ears or punch my ribs. He'd be shamed by Piers and Fergus for my catch. They both loved hare, and all Steffan had brought home lately were bony hole weasels.

It wasn't until I was halfway home that I realized I had forgotten to ask Morrighan why

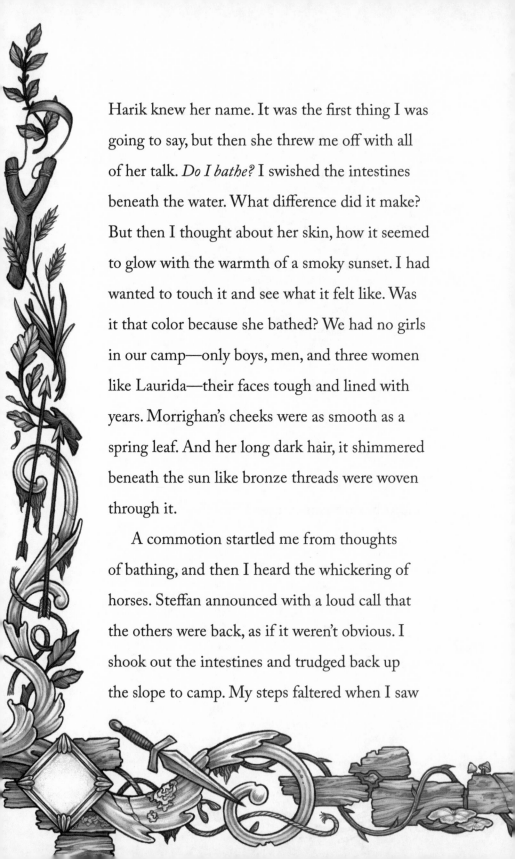

Harik knew her name. It was the first thing I was going to say, but then she threw me off with all of her talk. *Do I bathe?* I swished the intestines beneath the water. What difference did it make? But then I thought about her skin, how it seemed to glow with the warmth of a smoky sunset. I had wanted to touch it and see what it felt like. Was it that color because she bathed? We had no girls in our camp—only boys, men, and three women like Laurida—their faces tough and lined with years. Morrighan's cheeks were as smooth as a spring leaf. And her long dark hair, it shimmered beneath the sun like bronze threads were woven through it.

A commotion startled me from thoughts of bathing, and then I heard the whickering of horses. Steffan announced with a loud call that the others were back, as if it weren't obvious. I shook out the intestines and trudged back up the slope to camp. My steps faltered when I saw

Harik with the elders of the clan. He didn't come by our camp as often these days, instead staying in his massive fortress on the other side of the river—the one he had named Venda after his bride, the Siarrah. But the water was rising and the bridge was leaning. It might not be long before his fortress was cut off from the rest of us and he couldn't come at all. Fergus said the river would swallow the bridge soon. Harik balked and said he would build another, which seemed an impossible task, but he was larger in power and hunger than most, and it was rumored that his father had been one of the mightiest Ancients. Maybe he had ways we didn't know of.

"You remember the boy, don't you?" Fergus said, pointing at me.

"Steffan," Harik said, clamping his massive hand down on my shoulder.

"That's my brother. I'm Jafir," I said, but he

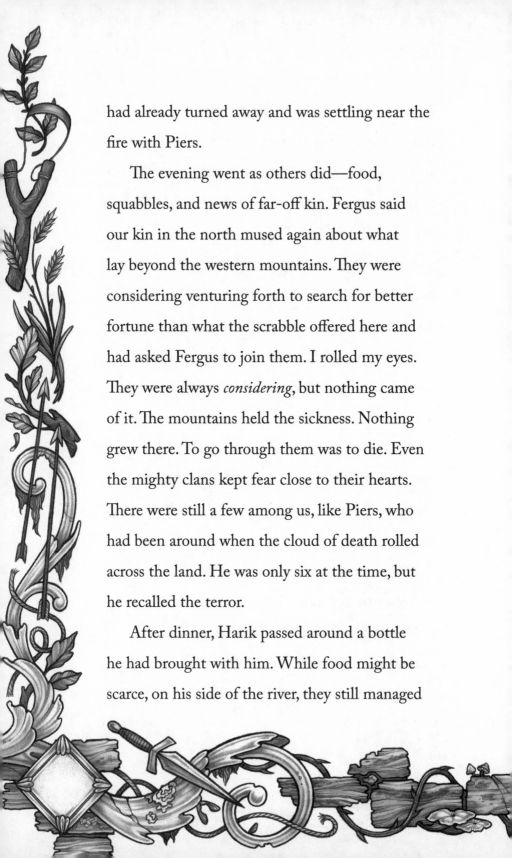

had already turned away and was settling near the fire with Piers.

The evening went as others did—food, squabbles, and news of far-off kin. Fergus said our kin in the north mused again about what lay beyond the western mountains. They were considering venturing forth to search for better fortune than what the scrabble offered here and had asked Fergus to join them. I rolled my eyes. They were always *considering*, but nothing came of it. The mountains held the sickness. Nothing grew there. To go through them was to die. Even the mighty clans kept fear close to their hearts. There were still a few among us, like Piers, who had been around when the cloud of death rolled across the land. He was only six at the time, but he recalled the terror.

After dinner, Harik passed around a bottle he had brought with him. While food might be scarce, on his side of the river, they still managed to brew the foul liquid. Even though I sat at the ring with everyone else, none was offered to me. Piers reached past me to hand the bottle to Reeve, who sat on my other side. I tried to act like I hadn't noticed when Harik passed the bottle on to Steffan. He drank and choked on the spirits, and everyone laughed. I did too, but Steffan plucked my laughter out from the rest. He turned and glared at me, the kind of glare that said I would pay later.

Then the talk turned to the tribes. Harik wondered, as he had on past visits, where one tribe in particular had gone. They hadn't been seen in four years. The Tribe of Gaudrel. When he said her name, I heard anger in his voice. "And that brat she drags with her," he added. "Morrighan."

I saw the hunger in his eyes. He wanted her. The most powerful man in the land—more powerful than Fergus—wanted Morrighan.

And I was the only one who knew where she was.

CHAPTER SEVEN

ℳORRIGHAN

HE DIDN'T HIDE IN THE BUSHES THIS TIME. HE strode up the wide marble steps in a frightening way. As if he owned them. Why was this scavenger so hard to understand? His chest was bare, and his face gleamed. He had bathed. With the dirt washed away, his skin was now a golden hue, and his long ropes of hair brighter. The broadening of his shoulders made his meatless ribs look more pathetic. But the look in his eyes was fierce.

"I thought you weren't coming?" I said, rising to meet him when he stopped in front of me.

He eyed me for a long while before answering. "I come and go, when and where I please. Why

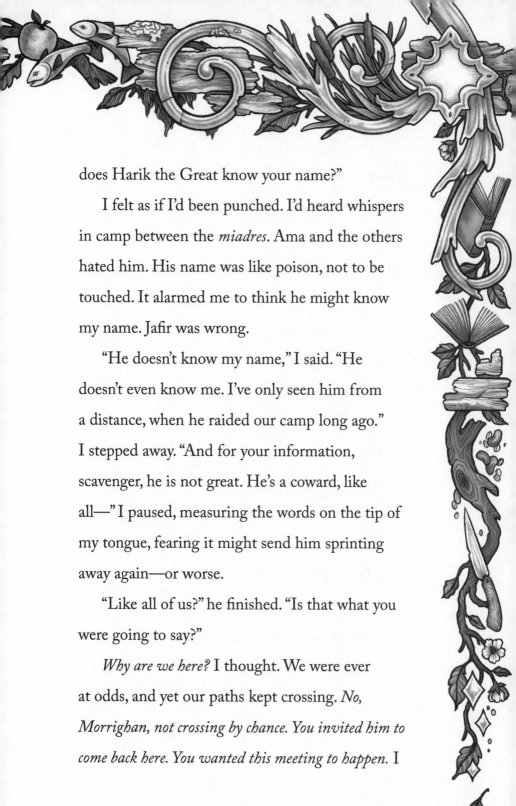

does Harik the Great know your name?"

I felt as if I'd been punched. I'd heard whispers
in camp between the *miadres*. Ama and the others
hated him. His name was like poison, not to be
touched. It alarmed me to think he might know
my name. Jafir was wrong.

"He doesn't know my name," I said. "He
doesn't even know me. I've only seen him from
a distance, when he raided our camp long ago."
I stepped away. "And for your information,
scavenger, he is not great. He's a coward, like
all—" I paused, measuring the words on the tip of
my tongue, fearing it might send him sprinting
away again—or worse.

"Like all of us?" he finished. "Is that what you
were going to say?"

Why are we here? I thought. We were ever
at odds, and yet our paths kept crossing. *No,
Morrighan, not crossing by chance. You invited him to
come back here. You wanted this meeting to happen.* I

didn't understand myself, nor all I had been taught to rely on. The scavengers were dangerous to our kind, but I was intensely curious about this one, who had shown me mercy six years ago when he was little more than a child himself.

"Jafir," I replied, saying his name with respect, "would you like to read?" And then, as a sign of truce, I added his own description. "A book of the *Ancients*?"

We read for an hour before he had to go. It wasn't our last meeting. The first few continued to be rocky and tentative. Scavengers and those they hunted had no common ground. But here, hidden away by long trails and box canyons, we learned to leave at least part of who we were behind us. Our trust ebbed and grew in turbulent starts, but it was always an unstated agreement that our meetings would remain a secret. If he told anyone, I could die. If I told anyone, I would be forbidden to return.

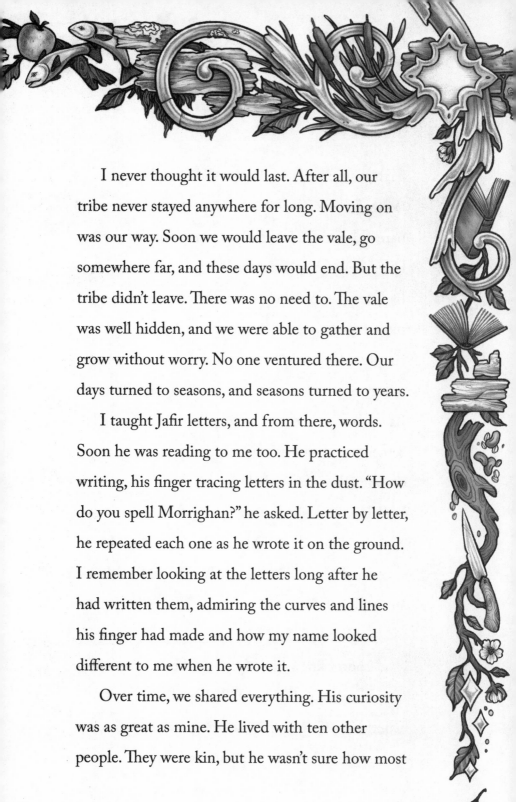

I never thought it would last. After all, our tribe never stayed anywhere for long. Moving on was our way. Soon we would leave the vale, go somewhere far, and these days would end. But the tribe didn't leave. There was no need to. The vale was well hidden, and we were able to gather and grow without worry. No one ventured there. Our days turned to seasons, and seasons turned to years.

I taught Jafir letters, and from there, words. Soon he was reading to me too. He practiced writing, his finger tracing letters in the dust. "How do you spell Morrighan?" he asked. Letter by letter, he repeated each one as he wrote it on the ground. I remember looking at the letters long after he had written them, admiring the curves and lines his finger had made and how my name looked different to me when he wrote it.

Over time, we shared everything. His curiosity was as great as mine. He lived with ten other people. They were kin, but he wasn't sure how most

of them were related. Fergus didn't explain such things to him. They weren't important. A woman named Laurida claimed him as her son, but he knew it wasn't so. She was Fergus's wife, but she hadn't come to the clan until Jafir was seven years old—from where, he wasn't sure. One day she'd simply ridden in with Fergus and stayed. He had a hazy memory of a woman he thought might have been his mother, but it was only her voice he remembered, not her face.

He asked if Gaudrel was my mother. I explained that she was my grandmother, a term he didn't know. "My mother's mother," I explained. "Ama raised me. My own mother died in childbirth."

"And your father?"

"I never knew him. Ama says he is dead too."

Jafir's lips pulled tight. Perhaps he was wondering if my father had died at the hands of one of his kin. He probably had. Ama would

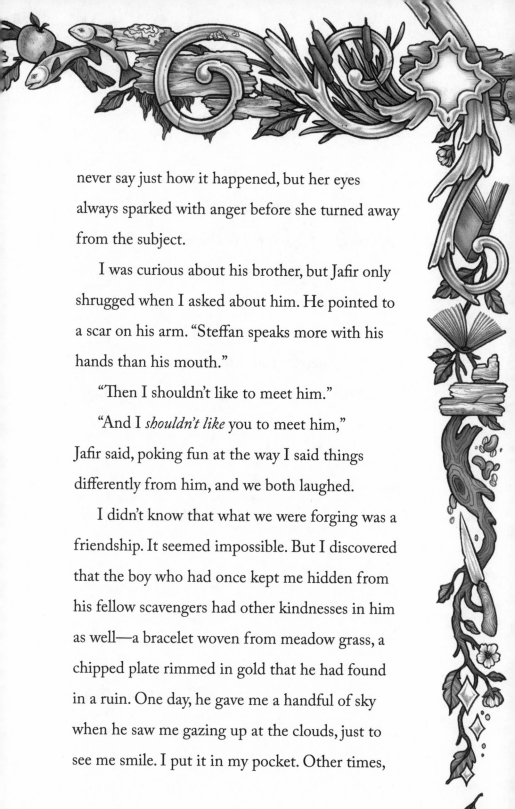

never say just how it happened, but her eyes
always sparked with anger before she turned away
from the subject.

I was curious about his brother, but Jafir only
shrugged when I asked about him. He pointed to
a scar on his arm. "Steffan speaks more with his
hands than his mouth."

"Then I shouldn't like to meet him."

"And I *shouldn't like* you to meet him,"
Jafir said, poking fun at the way I said things
differently from him, and we both laughed.

I didn't know that what we were forging was a
friendship. It seemed impossible. But I discovered
that the boy who had once kept me hidden from
his fellow scavengers had other kindnesses in him
as well—a bracelet woven from meadow grass, a
chipped plate rimmed in gold that he had found
in a ruin. One day, he gave me a handful of sky
when he saw me gazing up at the clouds, just to
see me smile. I put it in my pocket. Other times,

we maddened each other beyond telling with
our different ways, but we always came back,
our squabble forgotten. We changed together,
imperceptibly, day by day, as slowly as a tree
budding with spring.

But then one day, everything changed in a
single leap, permanently and forever.

He had stunned a squirrel that morning from
ten paces with his slingshot and was trying to
instruct me how to do the same, but shot after
shot, my stones went miserably off course. He
was chiding me for my aim, and I was leveling
frustrated glares at him.

"No, not like that," he complained. He jumped
up from where he lay in the meadow and marched
over to me. "Like *this*," he said, standing behind
me and wrapping his arms around mine. He took
my hands in his, his chest against my back, slowly
pulling the sling taut. Then he paused. A long,
uncomfortable pause that seemed to last forever,

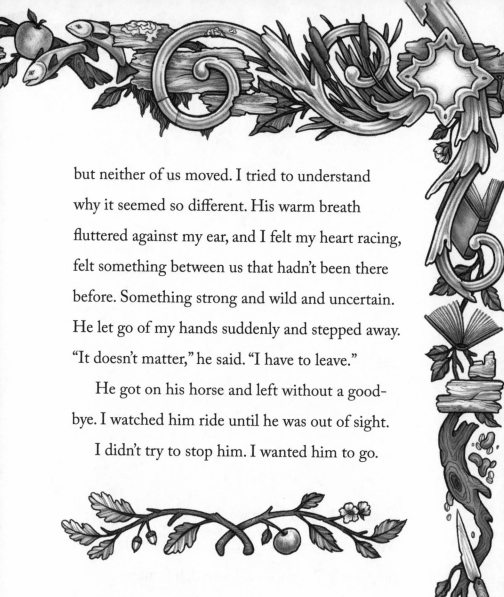

but neither of us moved. I tried to understand why it seemed so different. His warm breath fluttered against my ear, and I felt my heart racing, felt something between us that hadn't been there before. Something strong and wild and uncertain. He let go of my hands suddenly and stepped away. "It doesn't matter," he said. "I have to leave."

He got on his horse and left without a good-bye. I watched him ride until he was out of sight.

I didn't try to stop him. I wanted him to go.

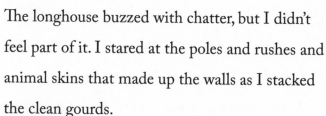

The longhouse buzzed with chatter, but I didn't feel part of it. I stared at the poles and rushes and animal skins that made up the walls as I stacked the clean gourds.

"You've hardly said a word all night. What's wrong, child?"

I whirled. "I'm not a child, Ama!" I snapped. "Can't you see that?" I sucked in a quick breath, startled by my own outburst.

Ama took the gourds from my hands and set them aside. "Yes," she said softly. "The child in you is gone, and a . . . young woman stands before me." Her pale gray eyes glistened. "I just refused to see. I'm not sure how it happened so fast."

I fell into her arms, holding her tight. "I'm sorry, Ama. I didn't mean to be short with you. I—"

But I had no more words to explain myself. My mind tossed and pitched, and my body no longer felt like my own. Instead, hot fingers squeezed my gut with the memory of Jafir's warm breath on my skin.

"I'm all right," I said. "The others wait."

Ama pulled me to the center of the longhouse, where everyone had settled around the fire. I sat down between Micah and Brynna. He was

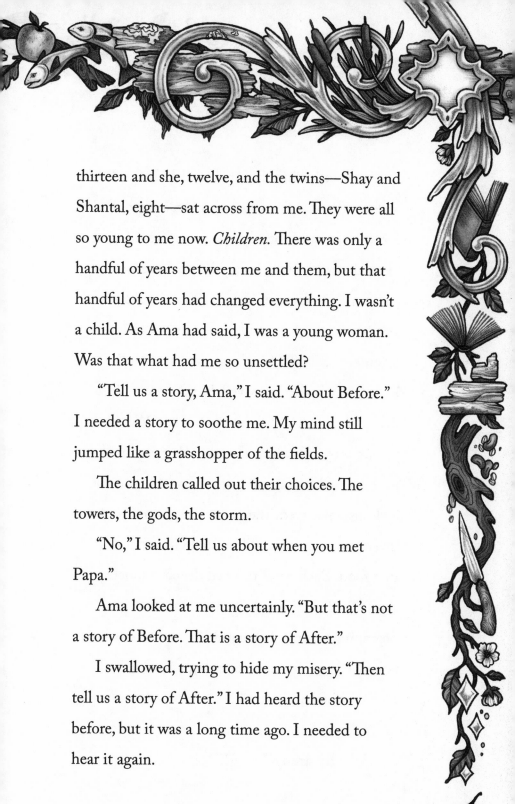

thirteen and she, twelve, and the twins—Shay and Shantal, eight—sat across from me. They were all so young to me now. *Children.* There was only a handful of years between me and them, but that handful of years had changed everything. I wasn't a child. As Ama had said, I was a young woman. Was that what had me so unsettled?

"Tell us a story, Ama," I said. "About Before." I needed a story to soothe me. My mind still jumped like a grasshopper of the fields.

The children called out their choices. The towers, the gods, the storm.

"No," I said. "Tell us about when you met Papa."

Ama looked at me uncertainly. "But that's not a story of Before. That is a story of After."

I swallowed, trying to hide my misery. "Then tell us a story of After." I had heard the story before, but it was a long time ago. I needed to hear it again.

Ama settled into her spot as she always did, rocking one way first, then another, a signal for everyone to quiet, briefly looking up, as if trying to recall a story, but I knew she held every story ready and close to her heart. "It was twelve years after the storm," she said. "I was only a girl of seventeen. By then I had traveled far with the Remnant who had survived, but only to a place that looked just as desolate as the last. We lived by our wits and will, my mother showing me how to trust the language of knowing within me, for little else mattered. The maps and gadgets and inventions of man could not help us survive or find food. Each day I reached deeper, unlocking the skills the gods had given us since the beginning of time. I thought this was all my life would ever be, but then one day, I saw him—"

"Was he handsome?"

"Oh, yes."

"Was he strong?"

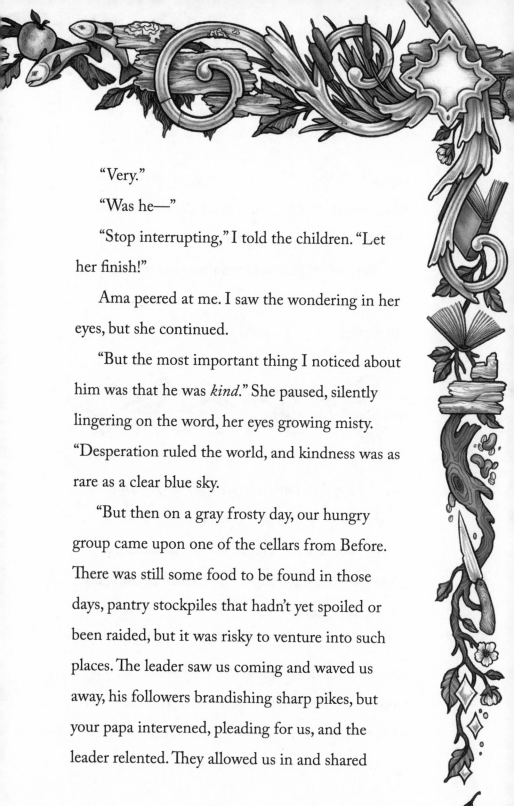

"Very."

"Was he—"

"Stop interrupting," I told the children. "Let her finish!"

Ama peered at me. I saw the wondering in her eyes, but she continued.

"But the most important thing I noticed about him was that he was *kind*." She paused, silently lingering on the word, her eyes growing misty. "Desperation ruled the world, and kindness was as rare as a clear blue sky.

"But then on a gray frosty day, our hungry group came upon one of the cellars from Before. There was still some food to be found in those days, pantry stockpiles that hadn't yet spoiled or been raided, but it was risky to venture into such places. The leader saw us coming and waved us away, his followers brandishing sharp pikes, but your papa intervened, pleading for us, and the leader relented. They allowed us in and shared

what little food there was. It was the last time I ever tasted an olive, but that small taste was the beginning of something far more . . . satisfying."

Pata rolled her eyes, and the other *miadres* laughed. *Far more.* The hidden meanings of Ama's stories no longer escaped me.

"Where are you off to in such a hurry?" Ama asked. "The beetles of the field will take you to task if you're late?" Her tone held suspicion. I had seen her watching me as I raced through my morning chores.

I slowed my steps, ashamed that I hadn't told Ama about the building of books—or Jafir. But not so ashamed that I came forth with the truth. One thing I had learned was that Ama could not read my mind as I had once believed. But she

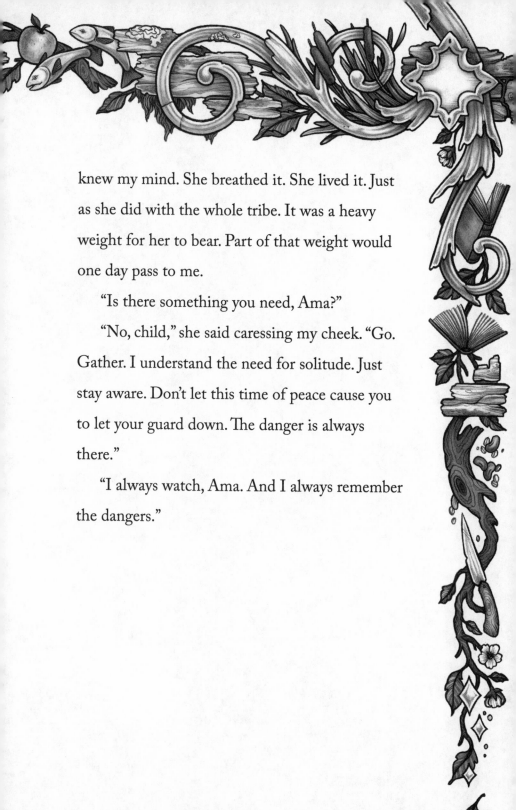

knew my mind. She breathed it. She lived it. Just as she did with the whole tribe. It was a heavy weight for her to bear. Part of that weight would one day pass to me.

"Is there something you need, Ama?"

"No, child," she said caressing my cheek. "Go. Gather. I understand the need for solitude. Just stay aware. Don't let this time of peace cause you to let your guard down. The danger is always there."

"I always watch, Ama. And I always remember the dangers."

CHAPTER EIGHT

MORRIGHAN

I FLEW THROUGH THE FIELDS. RAN BREATHLESSLY
down the canyon. The day was already hot, and
sweat rolled down my back. I stopped to gather
nothing, my empty bag flopping wildly in my
fist. When I reached the trail that led to the old
building of books, I saw his horse tied to the low
branch of a tree. And then I saw him.

He stood in the middle of the wide porch
entrance between two pillars, watching me
approach. He was early, just as I was. I slowed at
the base of the steps, catching my breath. I looked
at him in a way I never had before—in a way I
hadn't allowed myself to see him. How tall he had

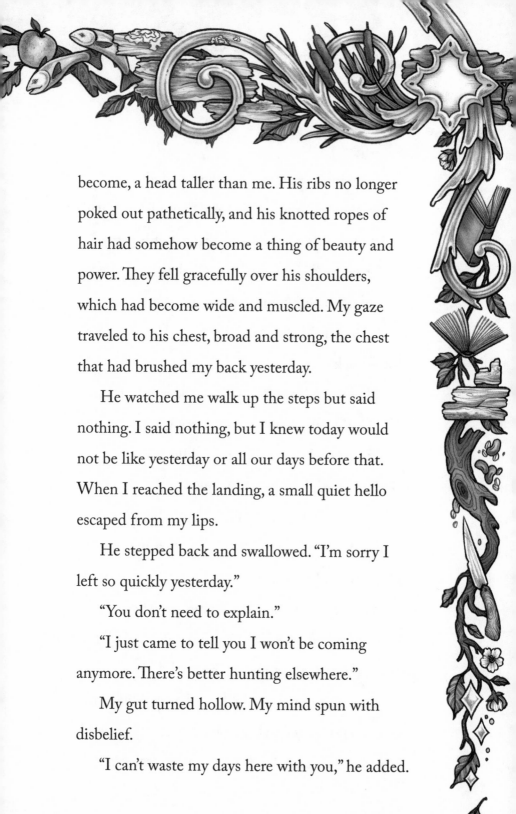

become, a head taller than me. His ribs no longer poked out pathetically, and his knotted ropes of hair had somehow become a thing of beauty and power. They fell gracefully over his shoulders, which had become wide and muscled. My gaze traveled to his chest, broad and strong, the chest that had brushed my back yesterday.

He watched me walk up the steps but said nothing. I said nothing, but I knew today would not be like yesterday or all our days before that. When I reached the landing, a small quiet hello escaped from my lips.

He stepped back and swallowed. "I'm sorry I left so quickly yesterday."

"You don't need to explain."

"I just came to tell you I won't be coming anymore. There's better hunting elsewhere."

My gut turned hollow. My mind spun with disbelief.

"I can't waste my days here with you," he added.

In a single beat, my disbelief ignited into
anger. I glared at him. "Because being friends with
a girl of the Remnant is one thing, but being—"

"You don't know me!" he yelled as he pushed
past me, hurtling himself down the steps.

"Go, Jafir!" I shouted after him. "Go and never
come back!"

He untied his horse with quick, angry jerks.

"Go!" I yelled, my vision blurring.

He paused, staring at the saddle, his hands
clamped in tight fury on his reins.

My heart pounded painfully in a long hopeful
beat, waiting. He shook his head, then mounted
his horse and rode away.

Whatever air was in my lungs vanished.

I stumbled back into the ruin, my hand gliding
along the wall for support. The cool darkness
swallowed me up. I reached a pillar and slid to the
ground, no longer trying to hold back my tears.
My thoughts tumbled between grief, resentment,

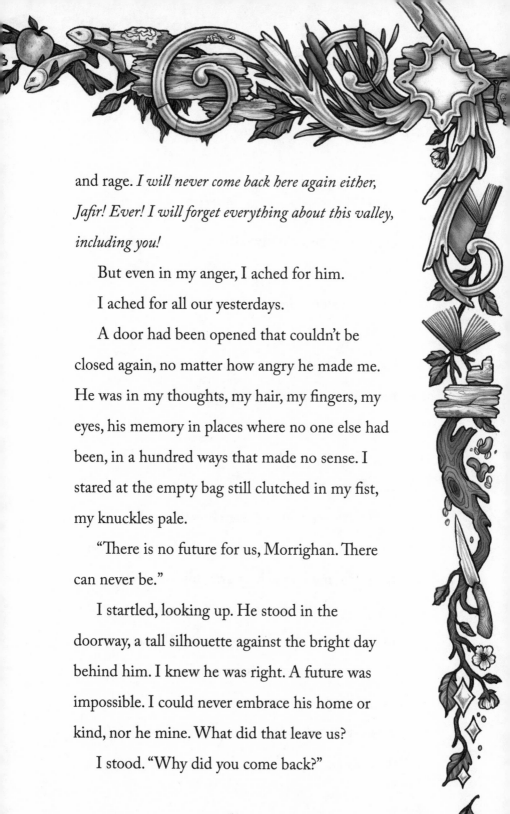

and rage. *I will never come back here again either, Jafir! Ever! I will forget everything about this valley, including you!*

But even in my anger, I ached for him.

I ached for all our yesterdays.

A door had been opened that couldn't be closed again, no matter how angry he made me. He was in my thoughts, my hair, my fingers, my eyes, his memory in places where no one else had been, in a hundred ways that made no sense. I stared at the empty bag still clutched in my fist, my knuckles pale.

"There is no future for us, Morrighan. There can never be."

I startled, looking up. He stood in the doorway, a tall silhouette against the bright day behind him. I knew he was right. A future was impossible. I could never embrace his home or kind, nor he mine. What did that leave us?

I stood. "Why did you come back?"

He stepped into the coolness of the cavern.
"Because . . ." His brows pulled down, his eyes
becoming dark clouds, still angry. "Because I could
not leave."

He walked closer until only inches separated
us. His gaze was sharp and searching. There was
so much I didn't know about the ways between a
man and a woman, but I knew I wanted him. And
I knew he wanted me.

"Touch me, Jafir," I said. "Touch me the way
you did yesterday."

His chest rose in a deep breath and he
hesitated, but then he lifted a single finger, slowly
tracing a line up my bare arm, his eyes following
the path as if he was memorizing it, and then
the path turned and his finger traveled across
my collarbone, resting in the hollow of my neck.
Something bright and liquid and hot rushed
beneath my skin and through my chest. My fingers
went slack, and I dropped the bag still in my grip.

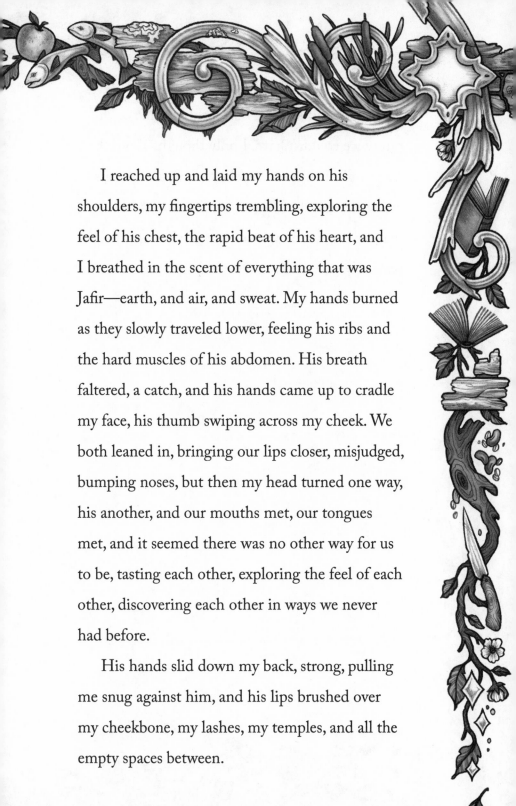

I reached up and laid my hands on his
shoulders, my fingertips trembling, exploring the
feel of his chest, the rapid beat of his heart, and
I breathed in the scent of everything that was
Jafir—earth, and air, and sweat. My hands burned
as they slowly traveled lower, feeling his ribs and
the hard muscles of his abdomen. His breath
faltered, a catch, and his hands came up to cradle
my face, his thumb swiping across my cheek. We
both leaned in, bringing our lips closer, misjudged,
bumping noses, but then my head turned one way,
his another, and our mouths met, our tongues
met, and it seemed there was no other way for us
to be, tasting each other, exploring the feel of each
other, discovering each other in ways we never
had before.

His hands slid down my back, strong, pulling
me snug against him, and his lips brushed over
my cheekbone, my lashes, my temples, and all the
empty spaces between.

I didn't think about his world or mine or the future we couldn't have. I only thought about the warm light behind my eyelids, his soft murmurs in my ear, and the fullness of what we had in that moment. And we touched in all the ways of yesterday and more.

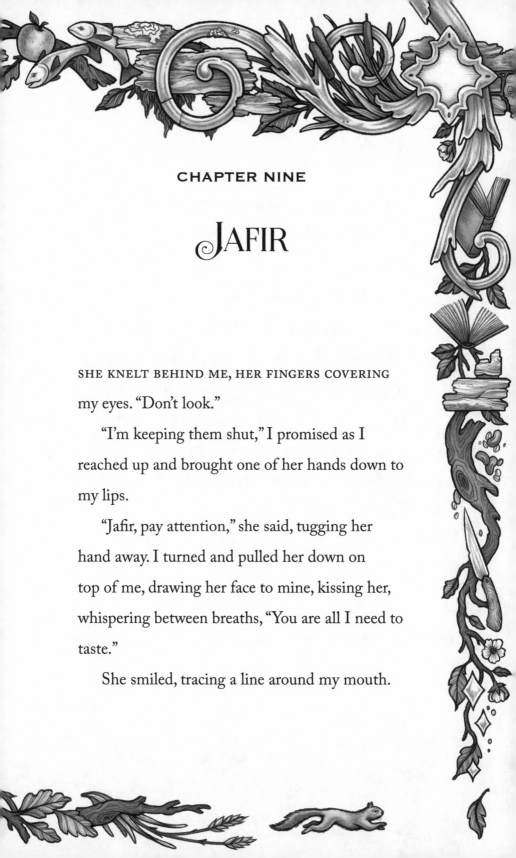

CHAPTER NINE

JAFIR

SHE KNELT BEHIND ME, HER FINGERS COVERING my eyes. "Don't look."

"I'm keeping them shut," I promised as I reached up and brought one of her hands down to my lips.

"Jafir, pay attention," she said, tugging her hand away. I turned and pulled her down on top of me, drawing her face to mine, kissing her, whispering between breaths, "You are all I need to taste."

She smiled, tracing a line around my mouth.

"But one day you will be glad for a berry to quench your thirst."

"You are—"

"Jafir!" she said, sitting up, straddling my stomach and placing a finger to my lips to quiet me.

I obediently closed my eyes.

I had asked her about the knowing, the gift the Siarrah of Harik the Great was said to have. She had frowned and said it was a gift to many in the tribes of the Remnant, except that some sought it more earnestly than others.

Here, she had told me, pressing her fist gently against my ribs.

And here, she said again, pressing it against my breastbone.

This is the same instruction my ama gave to me.
It is the language of knowing, Jafir.
A language as old as the universe itself.
It is seeing without eyes,

And listening without ears.
It is what led me here to this valley.
It is how the Ancients survived in those early years.
How we survive now.
Trust the strength within you.

Now she was determined to teach me this way of knowing.

She had already taught me much—the difference between berries that could nourish or kill, the seasons of the thannis weed, and stories of the gods who ruled it all. In the last few months, I hadn't missed a day of riding to the small concealed valley to be with her. She consumed my thoughts and dreams. Everything had changed between us the day she held my slingshot and I placed my arms around her. It frightened me, this change, the way it made me feel and even think differently, but every day since then, as I rode to the valley, all I could think of was holding her again, kissing her, listening to her, watching her laugh.

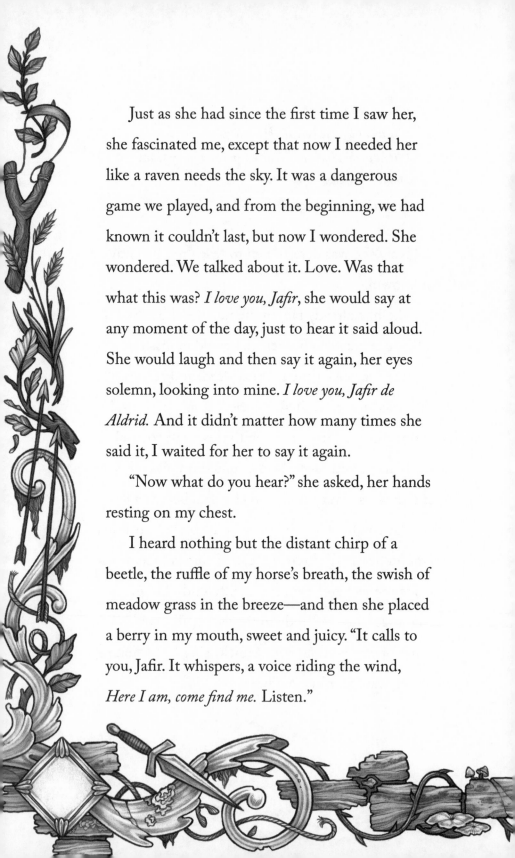

Just as she had since the first time I saw her, she fascinated me, except that now I needed her like a raven needs the sky. It was a dangerous game we played, and from the beginning, we had known it couldn't last, but now I wondered. She wondered. We talked about it. Love. Was that what this was? *I love you, Jafir*, she would say at any moment of the day, just to hear it said aloud. She would laugh and then say it again, her eyes solemn, looking into mine. *I love you, Jafir de Aldrid.* And it didn't matter how many times she said it, I waited for her to say it again.

"Now what do you hear?" she asked, her hands resting on my chest.

I heard nothing but the distant chirp of a beetle, the ruffle of my horse's breath, the swish of meadow grass in the breeze—and then she placed a berry in my mouth, sweet and juicy. "It calls to you, Jafir. It whispers, a voice riding the wind, *Here I am, come find me.* Listen."

But all I heard was a different kind of
knowing, one that even Morrighan couldn't hear,
a knowing that felt as sure and old as the earth
itself. It whispered deep within my gut, *I am yours,*
Morrighan, forever yours . . . and when the last star
of the universe blinks silent, I will still be yours.

CHAPTER TEN

MORRIGHAN

FROM THE TIME I WAS SMALL, AMA HAD TOLD
the stories of Before. Hundreds of stories.
Sometimes it was to prevent me from crying
and revealing our hiding place in the darkness
when the scavengers ranged too near, desperate
whispers in my ear that helped keep me silent.
More often, at the end of a long day, she told
them to satisfy me when there was no food to fill
my belly. *Stories are power*, she told me. *Hold them
close.*

I did. I clung to them, even if they were of a
world I didn't know, a world of sparkling light
and towers that reached to the sky, of kings

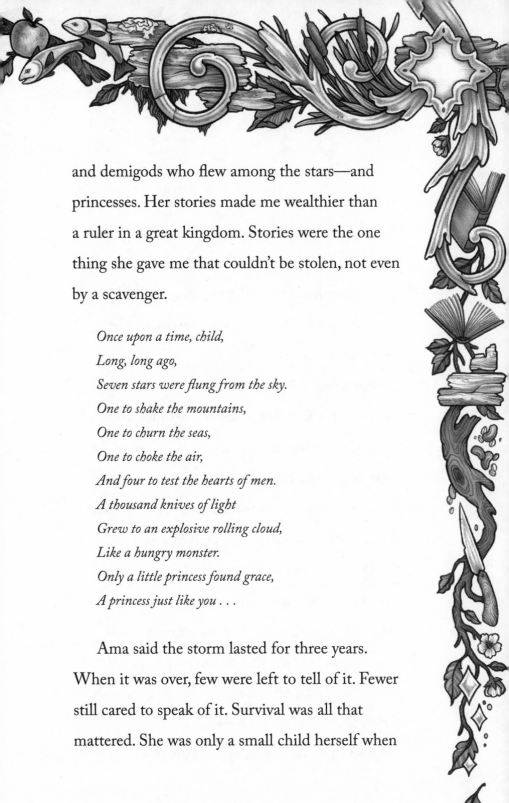

and demigods who flew among the stars—and princesses. Her stories made me wealthier than a ruler in a great kingdom. Stories were the one thing she gave me that couldn't be stolen, not even by a scavenger.

> *Once upon a time, child,*
> *Long, long ago,*
> *Seven stars were flung from the sky.*
> *One to shake the mountains,*
> *One to churn the seas,*
> *One to choke the air,*
> *And four to test the hearts of men.*
> *A thousand knives of light*
> *Grew to an explosive rolling cloud,*
> *Like a hungry monster.*
> *Only a little princess found grace,*
> *A princess just like you . . .*

Ama said the storm lasted for three years. When it was over, few were left to tell of it. Fewer still cared to speak of it. Survival was all that mattered. She was only a small child herself when

the storm began, her memory shaky, but she filled in the details with what she had learned along the way, and later more parts were added by the need of the moment. The message was always the same, though—a blessed Remnant survived— and they would always survive, no matter the hardship.

But other things survived too. Things we had to watch for. Things that sometimes made me doubt her words and our survival, like when Papa was struck down, trampled by a horse; when Venda was stolen; when Rhiann lost a baby goat and her life with the single slash of a knife.

These became stories too, and Ama charged us to tell them, saying, *We have already lost too much. We must never forget from where we came, lest we repeat history. Our stories must be passed to our sons and daughters, for with but one generation, history and truth are lost forever.*

And so I told the stories to Jafir as we

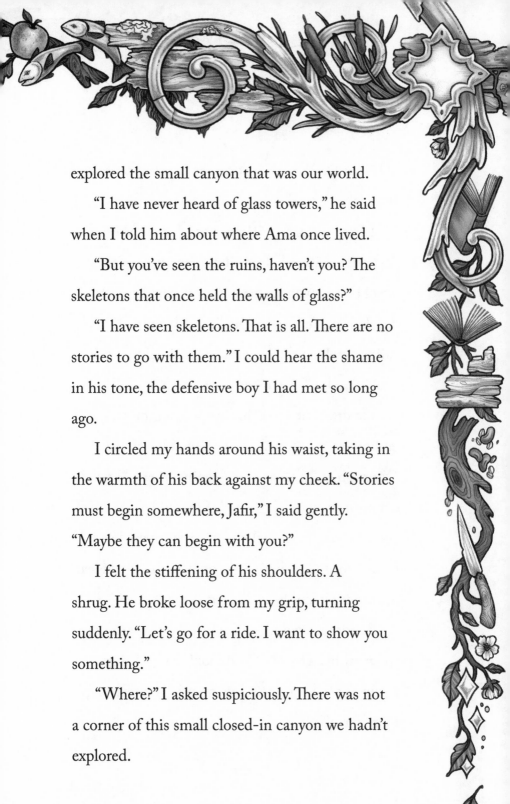

explored the small canyon that was our world.

"I have never heard of glass towers," he said when I told him about where Ama once lived.

"But you've seen the ruins, haven't you? The skeletons that once held the walls of glass?"

"I have seen skeletons. That is all. There are no stories to go with them." I could hear the shame in his tone, the defensive boy I had met so long ago.

I circled my hands around his waist, taking in the warmth of his back against my cheek. "Stories must begin somewhere, Jafir," I said gently. "Maybe they can begin with you?"

I felt the stiffening of his shoulders. A shrug. He broke loose from my grip, turning suddenly. "Let's go for a ride. I want to show you something."

"Where?" I asked suspiciously. There was not a corner of this small closed-in canyon we hadn't explored.

"Not far," he said, taking my hand. "I promise. It's a lake that—"

I frowned and pulled my hand away. We'd had this conversation before. The boundaries of the small box canyon seemed to grow smaller each day. Jafir chafed against its limits. He was used to riding freely in the open plains and fields, a risk I couldn't take. "Jafir, if someone sees me—"

He drew me close, his lips grazing mine, ending my words before they could be spoken. "Morrighan," he whispered against them, "I would cut out my own heart before I would let any harm come to you." He reached up, stroking my head. "I would not risk a single hair, or eyelash." He kissed me tenderly, and heat flooded through me.

Suddenly he jumped back, lifting his arms to show off his muscles. "And look!" he said, a grin teasing at the corners of his mouth. "I am strong! I am fierce!"

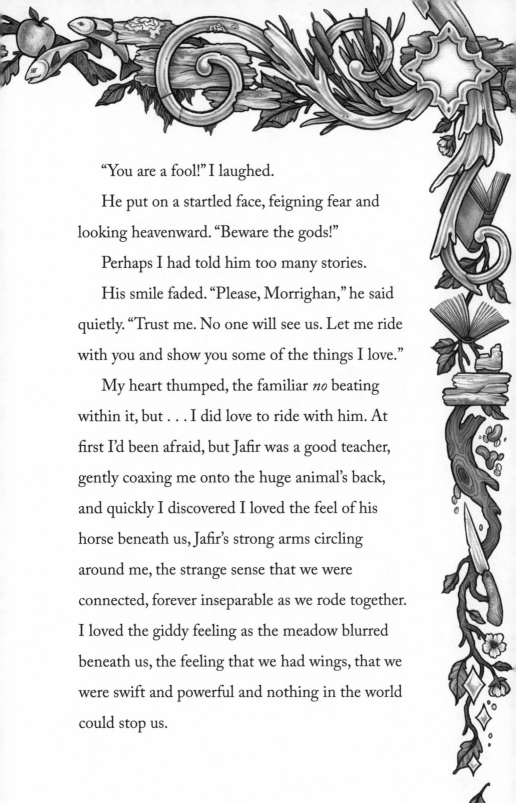

"You are a fool!" I laughed.

He put on a startled face, feigning fear and looking heavenward. "Beware the gods!"

Perhaps I had told him too many stories.

His smile faded. "Please, Morrighan," he said quietly. "Trust me. No one will see us. Let me ride with you and show you some of the things I love."

My heart thumped, the familiar *no* beating within it, but . . . I did love to ride with him. At first I'd been afraid, but Jafir was a good teacher, gently coaxing me onto the huge animal's back, and quickly I discovered I loved the feel of his horse beneath us, Jafir's strong arms circling around me, the strange sense that we were connected, forever inseparable as we rode together. I loved the giddy feeling as the meadow blurred beneath us, the feeling that we had wings, that we were swift and powerful and nothing in the world could stop us.

I looked at him and nodded. "Just this once," I
said.

"Just this once," he repeated.

But I knew I was opening another kind of
door, and like before, it was one that could never
be closed again.

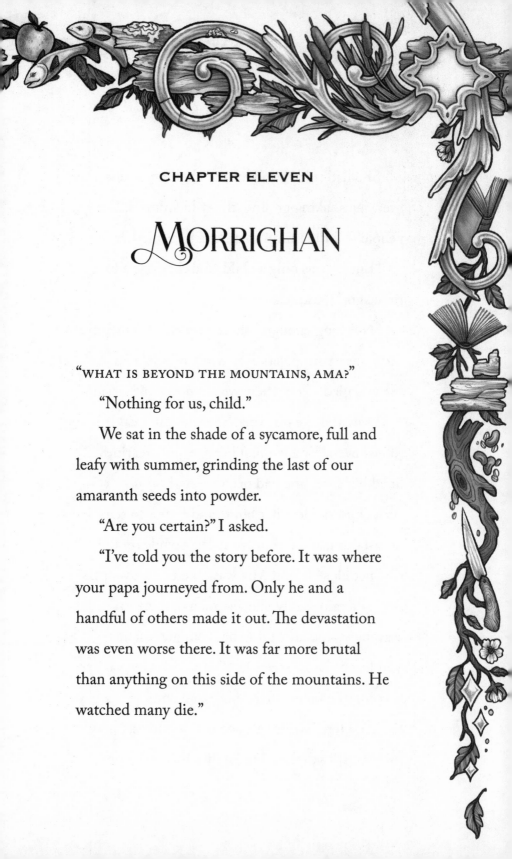

CHAPTER ELEVEN

MORRIGHAN

"WHAT IS BEYOND THE MOUNTAINS, AMA?"

"Nothing for us, child."

We sat in the shade of a sycamore, full and leafy with summer, grinding the last of our amaranth seeds into powder.

"Are you certain?" I asked.

"I've told you the story before. It was where your papa journeyed from. Only he and a handful of others made it out. The devastation was even worse there. It was far more brutal than anything on this side of the mountains. He watched many die."

She had told me about the choking clouds, the
fires, the shaking ground, the wild animals. The
people. All the things that Papa had told her.

"But he was only a child, and that was a long
time ago," I said.

"Not long enough," she answered. "I remember
the fear in your papa's eyes when he spoke of it.
He was glad to be where we are now, on this side."

I saw the age on Ama. She was still healthy,
robust even, for a woman her age, but weariness
lined her face. She had been through so much.
As a child she lost her home and father to the
devastation, and a short time later while on the
run, her close friend Mia was taken by scavengers
during a raid. Sadly, she lost many others to
scavengers too, including her younger sister,
Venda, and most recently, Rhiann. Moving on and
keeping the tribe safe had been an endless journey
for her. Here in this vale she had found rest now
for almost two years, but lately I had seen her

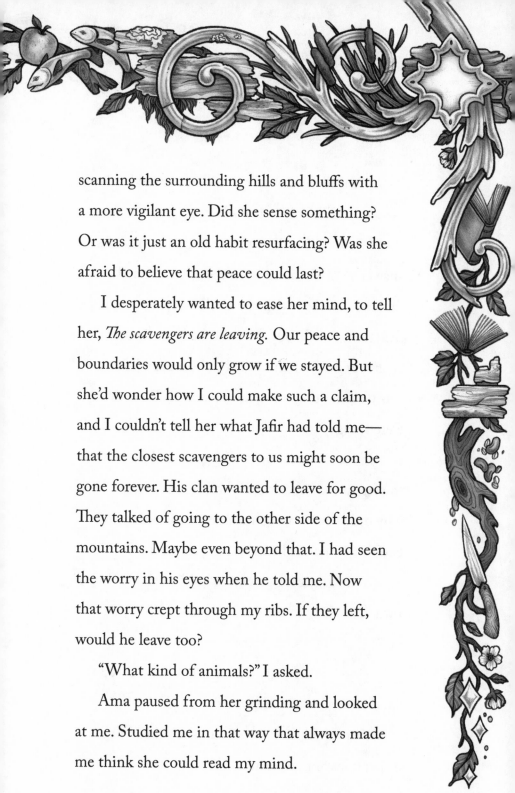

scanning the surrounding hills and bluffs with a more vigilant eye. Did she sense something? Or was it just an old habit resurfacing? Was she afraid to believe that peace could last?

I desperately wanted to ease her mind, to tell her, *The scavengers are leaving.* Our peace and boundaries would only grow if we stayed. But she'd wonder how I could make such a claim, and I couldn't tell her what Jafir had told me—that the closest scavengers to us might soon be gone forever. His clan wanted to leave for good. They talked of going to the other side of the mountains. Maybe even beyond that. I had seen the worry in his eyes when he told me. Now that worry crept through my ribs. If they left, would he leave too?

"What kind of animals?" I asked.

Ama paused from her grinding and looked at me. Studied me in that way that always made me think she could read my mind.

I glanced down and ground at my seeds more
earnestly. "I'm only curious."

"I don't know all of the animals' names," she
answered. "One he called a tiger. It was smaller
than a horse, but with the teeth of a wolf and
the strength of a bull. He watched one of the
creatures drag a man away by the leg, and there
was nothing they could do to stop it. The animals
were hungry too."

"If the Ancients were like gods and built
towers to the sky and flew among the stars,
why did they have such dangerous animals that
couldn't be controlled? Weren't they afraid?"

Ama's gray eyes turned to cold steel. Her head
turned slightly to the side. "What did you just
say?"

I stared at her, wondering what had caused the
sudden hardness in her voice.

"You called them *Ancients*," she said. "Where
did you learn that term?"

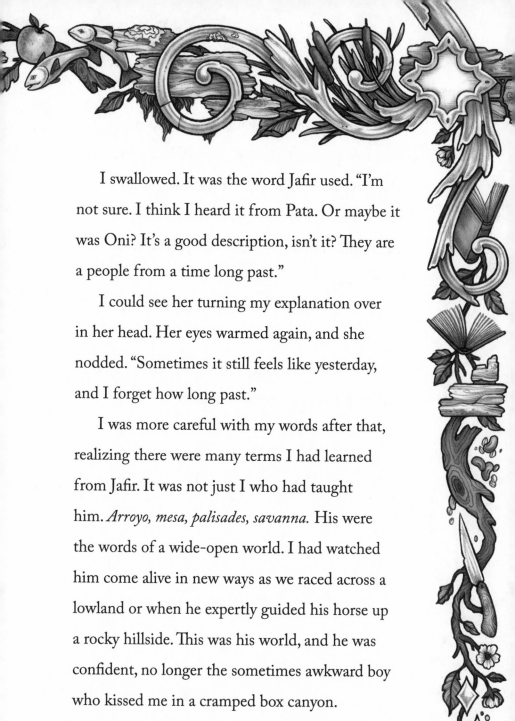

I swallowed. It was the word Jafir used. "I'm not sure. I think I heard it from Pata. Or maybe it was Oni? It's a good description, isn't it? They are a people from a time long past."

I could see her turning my explanation over in her head. Her eyes warmed again, and she nodded. "Sometimes it still feels like yesterday, and I forget how long past."

I was more careful with my words after that, realizing there were many terms I had learned from Jafir. It was not just I who had taught him. *Arroyo, mesa, palisades, savanna.* His were the words of a wide-open world. I had watched him come alive in new ways as we raced across a lowland or when he expertly guided his horse up a rocky hillside. This was his world, and he was confident, no longer the sometimes awkward boy who kissed me in a cramped box canyon.

I came alive with him, allowing myself to believe, however briefly, that it was my world

too, that our dreams lay just over the next hill, or the next, and we had wings to take us there. But I always watched over my shoulder, always remembered who I was, and where I was destined to return, a hidden world where Jafir would never fit in.

There is no future for us, Morrighan. There can never be.

Jafir had a knowing about him too. It was a knowing I didn't want to think about.

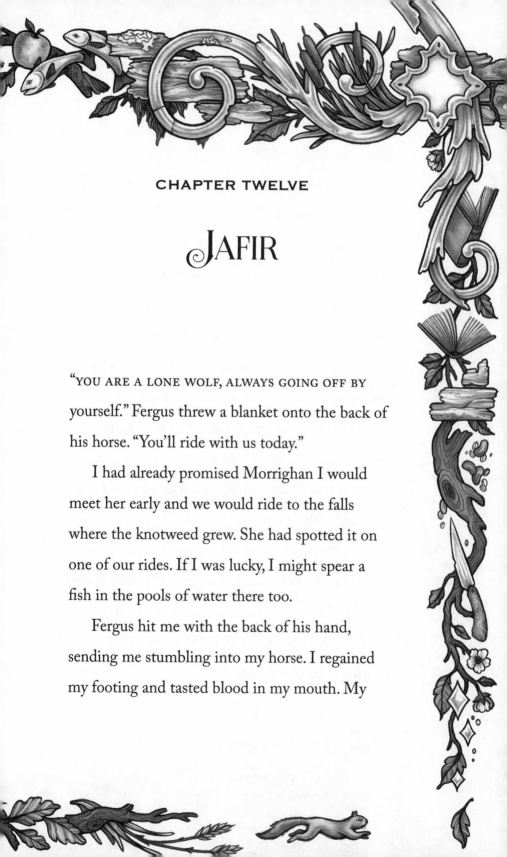

CHAPTER TWELVE

JAFIR

"YOU ARE A LONE WOLF, ALWAYS GOING OFF BY yourself." Fergus threw a blanket onto the back of his horse. "You'll ride with us today."

I had already promised Morrighan I would meet her early and we would ride to the falls where the knotweed grew. She had spotted it on one of our rides. If I was lucky, I might spear a fish in the pools of water there too.

Fergus hit me with the back of his hand, sending me stumbling into my horse. I regained my footing and tasted blood in my mouth. My

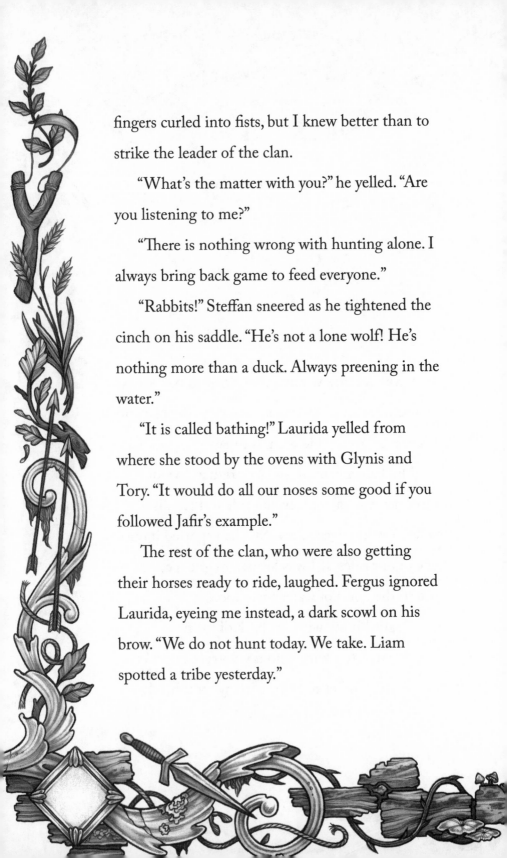

fingers curled into fists, but I knew better than to strike the leader of the clan.

"What's the matter with you?" he yelled. "Are you listening to me?"

"There is nothing wrong with hunting alone. I always bring back game to feed everyone."

"Rabbits!" Steffan sneered as he tightened the cinch on his saddle. "He's not a lone wolf! He's nothing more than a duck. Always preening in the water."

"It is called bathing!" Laurida yelled from where she stood by the ovens with Glynis and Tory. "It would do all our noses some good if you followed Jafir's example."

The rest of the clan, who were also getting their horses ready to ride, laughed. Fergus ignored Laurida, eyeing me instead, a dark scowl on his brow. "We do not hunt today. We take. Liam spotted a tribe yesterday."

My veins turned to fire. "A tribe?" I asked. "*Where?*"

He mistook my quick reply for eagerness and smiled. It was a rare sight on his face, especially if it was directed at me. "An hour's ride north," he answered. "Their bellies were fat, and their baskets full."

I breathed relief. Morrighan's tribe was south of ours. Our clan hadn't raided a camp since last spring. The tribes had either become better at hiding or had moved far from us.

"You don't need me," I said, looking at Piers, Liam, and the rest. "You have enough—"

Fergus grabbed me by my shirt, jerking me close, his expression a threatening storm. "You ride with us. You are my son."

There would be no dissuading him. I nodded, and he released his grip. I stared after him as he mounted his horse, wondering what ate through

him. It was not like him to even remember that he was my father.

They did not fight back. It sickened me how easily their food was taken. It was a small tribe, only about nine, but none defended their ground. An iron poker lay near their fire, a knife on a rough wooden table, rocks at their feet, but none lifted hand or weapon toward us. *Fight back*, I wanted to say, but I knew if they did, we would cut them down. Not all of them, but enough to send the message. *Do not fight us. We are hungry like you, and we deserve this food as much as you, even if it was gathered by your hand.* It had always made sense to me before, but now the words seemed jumbled, different, as if they had been rearranged.

It is them or us. The whisper was faint now, and I wondered if I had ever heard it at all. I couldn't remember my mother's face anymore, not even the color of her hair, but I still felt her lips against my ear, warm, sickly, the sour smell of death on them, whispering the ways of our clan. *The tribes have a knowing about them, a way of conjuring food from the dry grasses of the hills. As the gods have blessed them, so should they bless us.*

I tied a sack of acorns to the back of my horse, while the rest of the clan pillaged or brandished their weapons as warning. I kept my gaze down, concentrating on tightening the rope, avoiding looking at any of them, but I couldn't ignore the whimpers of a few. These acorns, gathered by them, were no blessing to me, and the bile rose in my throat. My father's scornful words surfaced again. *What's the matter with you?* I saw the back of his hand again, felt the hot bruise rising on my face, the torn flesh inside my cheek. How could I expect them to fight back, when even I refused to defend myself?

Steffan eyed a girl cowering behind the older women of the tribe.

"Come here," he called to her.

She shook her head wildly, her wide eyes glistening. The women pulled closer, shoulder to shoulder.

"Come!" he ordered.

"We're finished here," I said, grabbing his arm. "Leave the girl alone."

"Stay out of it, Jafir!" he yelled. He threw off my arm, advancing toward her, but Piers stepped into his path.

"As your brother said, we are done." Steffan had come to blows with Piers before, but Fergus, Liam, and Reeve were already riding off. The others were also mounting their horses to leave.

Steffan glared at the girl. "I'll be back," he warned, and left with the rest of us.

We traveled swiftly over the grasslands and hills back to camp, and with each mile, my anger grew. *Fight back.* Conflicting words galloped in my head. *Them or us.*

By the time we got to camp, only one thing was certain to me.

I would never ride with them again.

I would see my kin starve first.

I returned to the raided camp the next day, alone, with two peafowl that had taken me all day to hunt down. All that remained of their camp were the cold ashes of a fire and scattered scraps left behind in haste.

The tribe had moved on to someplace where we wouldn't find them again, and I was glad to see them gone.

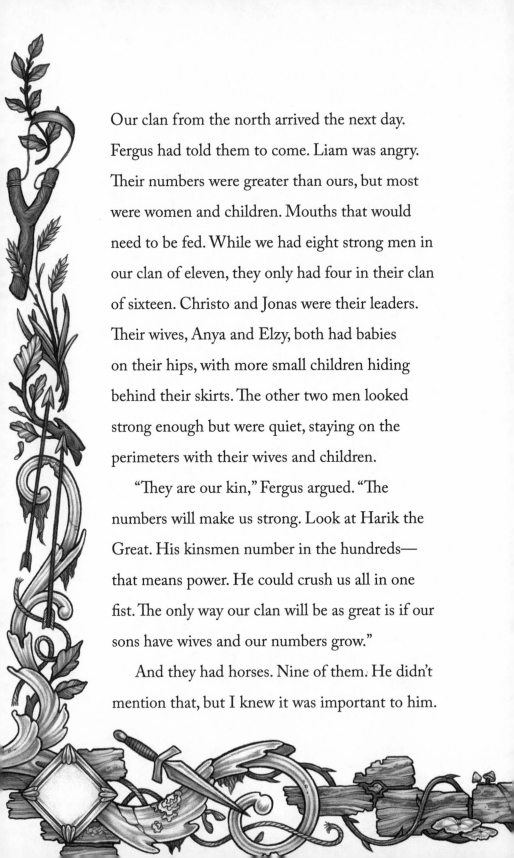

Our clan from the north arrived the next day. Fergus had told them to come. Liam was angry. Their numbers were greater than ours, but most were women and children. Mouths that would need to be fed. While we had eight strong men in our clan of eleven, they only had four in their clan of sixteen. Christo and Jonas were their leaders. Their wives, Anya and Elzy, both had babies on their hips, with more small children hiding behind their skirts. The other two men looked strong enough but were quiet, staying on the perimeters with their wives and children.

"They are our kin," Fergus argued. "The numbers will make us strong. Look at Harik the Great. His kinsmen number in the hundreds— that means power. He could crush us all in one fist. The only way our clan will be as great is if our sons have wives and our numbers grow."

And they had horses. Nine of them. He didn't mention that, but I knew it was important to him.

In his mind, horses were symbols of power too, even better than great stores of food. He knew exactly how many horses Harik had in his stables.

Liam argued there was barely enough food in the hills to feed our own.

"Then we will find new hills."

I looked at the children huddled together, too afraid to speak, their eyes circled with hunger and days of walking. Laurida poured water into the kettle over the fire to make the stew stretch and then added two large handfuls of the salted meat we had stolen from the tribe. The mother of one of the children began to cry. The sound cut through me, strangely familiar—*them or us*—and for a fleeting moment, I was glad for what we had stolen.

The evening passed, prickly and uncomfortable, the children eating quietly, the heated words between Liam and Fergus weighing on the rest, Liam still casting glares at

the newcomers. With their soup finished, the children and mothers stared glumly into the fire. The silence was stifling. I preferred squabbles and scuffles to the taut hush.

Anger welled in me, and I whispered to Laurida, "Why do we never tell stories?"

Laurida shrugged. "Stories are a luxury of the well-fed."

"At least stories would fill the silence!" I snapped. "Or help us understand our past!" And then lower, under my breath as I glared down at the ground: "I don't even know how my own mother died."

Fergus's boots suddenly filled my circle of vision. I looked up. His eyes blazed with anger. "She starved to death," he said. "She hid away her share of food and gave it to you and Steffan. She died because of you. Is *that* the story you wanted to hear?"

On a different night, I might have felt the back of his hand again, but his expression was so filled with disgust, the effort to hit me must not have seemed worth it, and he turned away.

No, it was not the story I wanted to hear.

CHAPTER THIRTEEN

MORRIGHAN

"WHERE WERE YOU?" I ASKED, RUNNING TO MEET him as he got off his horse. He hadn't come for three days, and I had feared the worst.

He drew me into his arms, holding me tight in a strange, desperate way.

"Jafir?"

He pulled back, and that's when I saw the side of his face, a purple bruise coloring it from cheekbone to jaw, and circling under his eye.

Fear skittered through my chest. "What beast did this?" I demanded, reaching for his cheek.

He brushed my hand away. "It is nothing."

"Jafir!" I insisted.

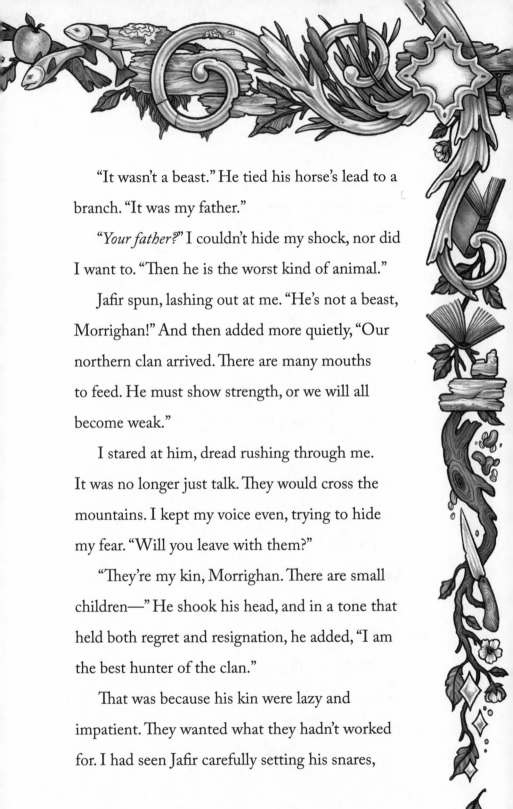

"It wasn't a beast." He tied his horse's lead to a branch. "It was my father."

"*Your father?*" I couldn't hide my shock, nor did I want to. "Then he is the worst kind of animal."

Jafir spun, lashing out at me. "He's not a beast, Morrighan!" And then added more quietly, "Our northern clan arrived. There are many mouths to feed. He must show strength, or we will all become weak."

I stared at him, dread rushing through me. It was no longer just talk. They would cross the mountains. I kept my voice even, trying to hide my fear. "Will you leave with them?"

"They're my kin, Morrighan. There are small children—" He shook his head, and in a tone that held both regret and resignation, he added, "I am the best hunter of the clan."

That was because his kin were lazy and impatient. They wanted what they hadn't worked for. I had seen Jafir carefully setting his snares,

patiently sharpening his arrows, scanning the grasses with the steady eye of a hawk, looking for the slightest rustle.

"Before they leave, you could teach them. You could—"

"I cannot stay in this canyon, Morrighan! Where would I go?"

I didn't need to say the words. He saw them in my eyes. *Come with me to my tribe.*

He shook his head. "I'm not like your kind." And then more sharply, almost as an accusation: "Why don't you carry weapons?"

I bristled, pulling back my shoulders. "We have weapons. We just don't use them on people."

"Maybe if you did, you wouldn't be so weak."

Weak? My fingers curled into a fist, and swifter than a hare, I punched him in the stomach. He grunted, doubling over.

"Does that seem weak to you, mighty

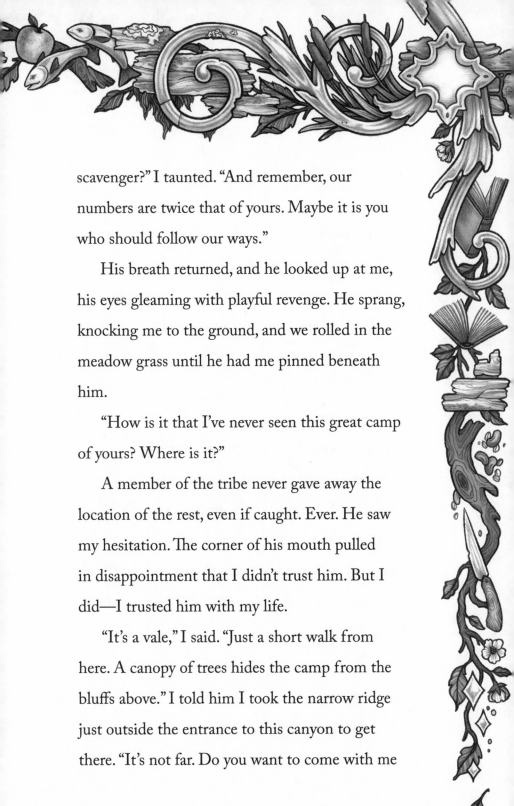

scavenger?" I taunted. "And remember, our numbers are twice that of yours. Maybe it is you who should follow our ways."

His breath returned, and he looked up at me, his eyes gleaming with playful revenge. He sprang, knocking me to the ground, and we rolled in the meadow grass until he had me pinned beneath him.

"How is it that I've never seen this great camp of yours? Where is it?"

A member of the tribe never gave away the location of the rest, even if caught. Ever. He saw my hesitation. The corner of his mouth pulled in disappointment that I didn't trust him. But I did—I trusted him with my life.

"It's a vale," I said. "Just a short walk from here. A canopy of trees hides the camp from the bluffs above." I told him I took the narrow ridge just outside the entrance to this canyon to get there. "It's not far. Do you want to come with me

to see it?" I asked, thinking he had changed his mind.

He shook his head. "With more mouths to feed, there is more hunting to be done."

A knot grew in my throat. His kin needed him. They would take him away from me. "Past the mountains there are animals, Jafir. There are—"

"Shh," he said, his finger resting on my lips. His hand spread out to gently cradle my face. "Morrighan, the girl of ponds and books and knowing." He stared at me like I was the air he breathed, the sun that warmed his back, even the stars that lit his way—a gaze that said, *I need you.* Or maybe those were all the things I wanted him to see in my eyes.

"Don't worry," he finally said. "We won't leave for a long while. More supplies need to be gathered for such a journey, and with so many mouths to feed, it is hard to save up. And some in

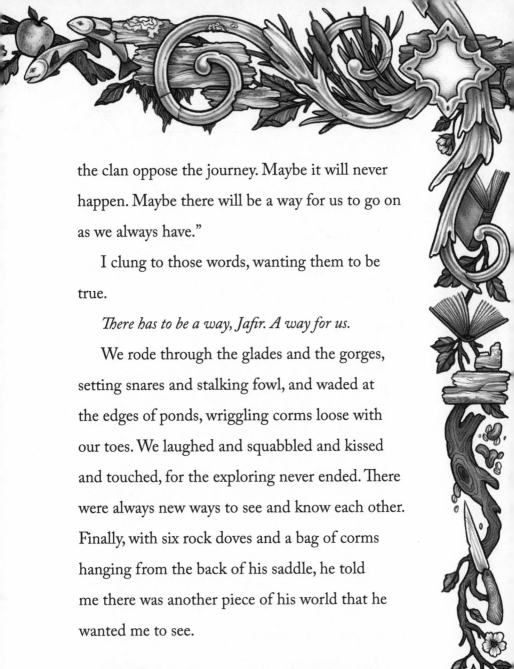

the clan oppose the journey. Maybe it will never happen. Maybe there will be a way for us to go on as we always have."

I clung to those words, wanting them to be true.

There has to be a way, Jafir. A way for us.

We rode through the glades and the gorges, setting snares and stalking fowl, and waded at the edges of ponds, wriggling corms loose with our toes. We laughed and squabbled and kissed and touched, for the exploring never ended. There were always new ways to see and know each other. Finally, with six rock doves and a bag of corms hanging from the back of his saddle, he told me there was another piece of his world that he wanted me to see.

"It's magnificent," I said. Strangely and bizarrely magnificent.

We stood on the edge of a shallow lake, the water lapping at our bare feet. Jafir stood behind me, his arms circling around my waist, his chin brushing my temple.

"I knew you would like it," he said. "There must be a story in this."

I couldn't imagine exactly what that would be, but it had to be a story of randomness and chance, of luck and destiny.

On a knoll in the middle of the lake was a door, surely part of something greater at one time, but the rest was long swept away—a home, a family, lives that mattered to someone. Gone. Somehow the door alone had survived, still hanging in its frame, an unlikely sentinel of another time. It swung in the breeze as if saying, *Remember. Remember me.*

The wood of the door was bleached as white

as the dried grass of summer. But the part that left me most in awe was a tiny window no bigger than my hand in the upper half of the door. It was made of red and green colored glass pieced together like a cluster of ripe berries.

"Why did that survive?" I asked.

Behind me, I felt Jafir gently shake his head. And then the afternoon sun dipped lower and the rays skipped through the panes just as Jafir promised they would, casting us in jeweled light.

I felt the magic of it, the fragile beauty of a moment that would soon be gone, and I wanted it to last forever. I turned in the circle of Jafir's arms and looked at the prism of light coloring his hair, the ridge of his lip, my hands on his shoulders, and I kissed him, thinking that perhaps one kind of magic might make another last forever.

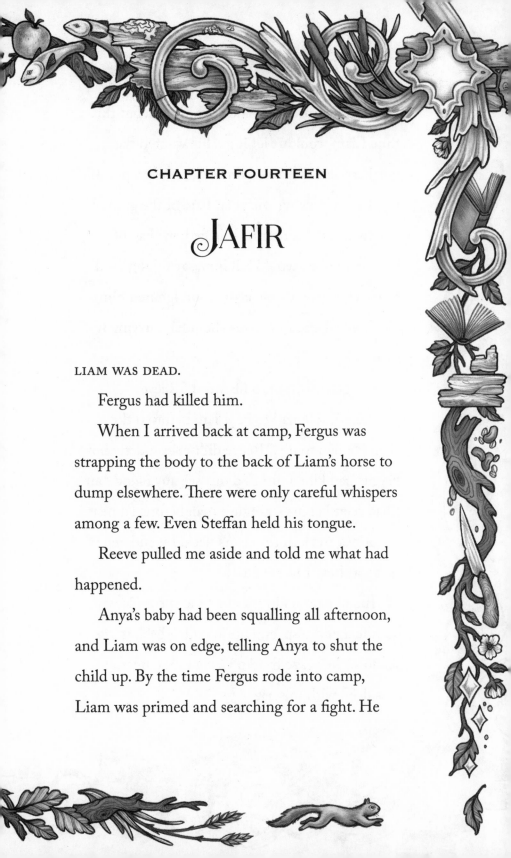

CHAPTER FOURTEEN

JAFIR

LIAM WAS DEAD.

Fergus had killed him.

When I arrived back at camp, Fergus was strapping the body to the back of Liam's horse to dump elsewhere. There were only careful whispers among a few. Even Steffan held his tongue.

Reeve pulled me aside and told me what had happened.

Anya's baby had been squalling all afternoon, and Liam was on edge, telling Anya to shut the child up. By the time Fergus rode into camp, Liam was primed and searching for a fight. He laid into Fergus again, and they argued, but this time Liam wouldn't let it go. He wanted the northern kin to leave and the clan to stay put. If not, he was leaving with his share of the grain. Fergus warned him if he touched one bag of the supplies, he would kill him, saying the food belonged to the whole clan. Liam ignored him and hoisted a bag onto his shoulder, carrying it toward his horse.

"Fergus was true to his word," Reeve whispered. "He had to be. Liam betrayed the clan. He had to die." Reeve didn't say exactly how Fergus had killed him. I didn't see any blood, but I had seen Fergus strangle a man before. I'd heard the bones crack in the man's neck. I wondered if that was how Liam died.

The northern kin watched the spectacle with both fear and respect. Laurida hung back in the shadows, her gaze fixed on Fergus, the lines at her eyes deep with misery.

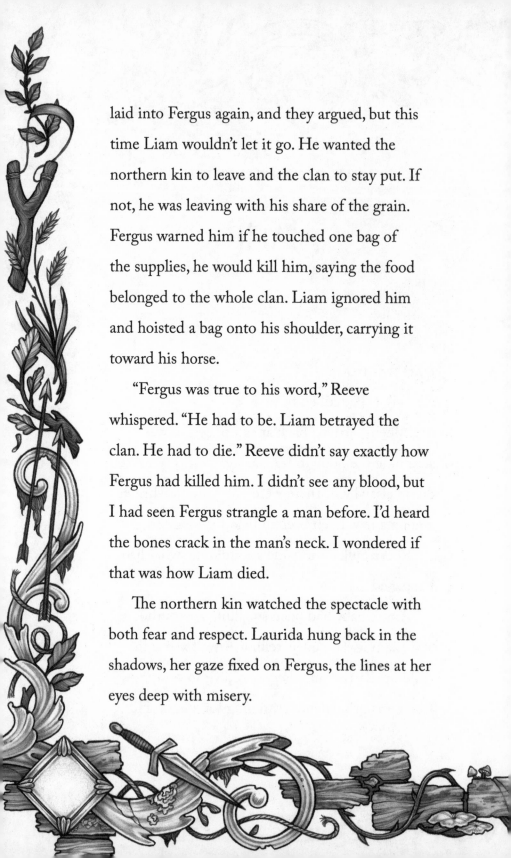

I looked at him, *my father*, pulling the strap
tight on Liam's body. Determined. Angry. His
silence said more than anything else. Liam was his
brother.

The evening wore especially long, the silence
growing like a thorny hedge between us, and after
the last of the children were put to bed and Fergus
had returned with Liam's empty horse, I headed
for my own bedroll.

Steffan shouldered me in passing as if by
accident. "Where were you all day, Jafir? *Hunting?*"

I turned, caught off guard by his question.
He never brought up my hunting, since I was the
most skilled at it.

"The same as every day," I answered. "Didn't
you see the game and food I brought back?"

He nodded. Then smiled. "So I did. Well done, little brother." He patted my back and walked away. I wondered if Steffan was drunk, but I hadn't smelled any of Harik's brew on his breath. Maybe crows had led him to some fermented berries.

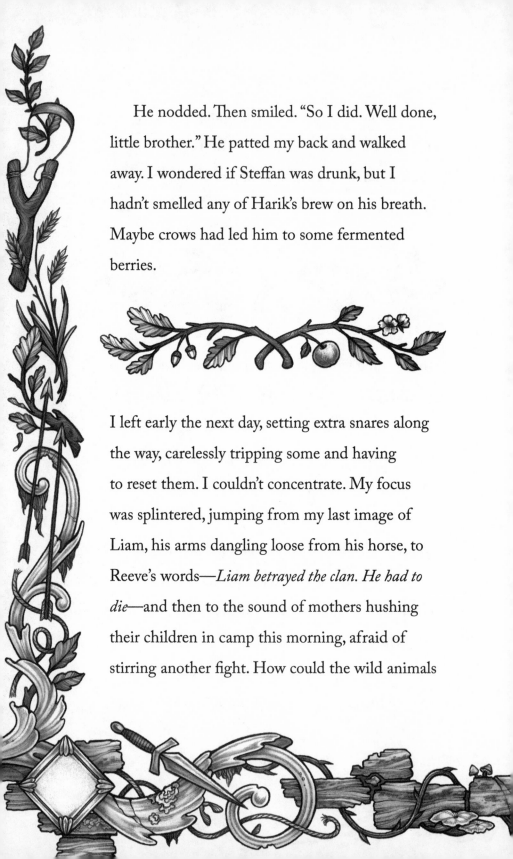

I left early the next day, setting extra snares along the way, carelessly tripping some and having to reset them. I couldn't concentrate. My focus was splintered, jumping from my last image of Liam, his arms dangling loose from his horse, to Reeve's words—*Liam betrayed the clan. He had to die*—and then to the sound of mothers hushing their children in camp this morning, afraid of stirring another fight. How could the wild animals that lived beyond the mountains be any worse than this? With the last trap set, I pushed my horse faster to get to Morrighan, blocking out the world, as if the wind rushing through my hair could erase what lay behind me.

CHAPTER FIFTEEN

MORRIGHAN

IT HAD BEEN A LONG MORNING, AND WORRY
needled through me as each hour passed. Though
I had finished my chores early—weeding the
garden, repairing the frayed baskets, and stripping
new rushes for the floor—when I told Ama I
was off to gather, she found yet another chore
for me, and another. Morning turned to midday.
My anxiety burned deeper as I watched her cast
glances toward the end of the vale, and when I
finally grabbed my bag to leave, she said, "Take
Brynna and Micah with you."

"No, Ama," I groaned. "I've worked with them
through every chore this morning, and neither

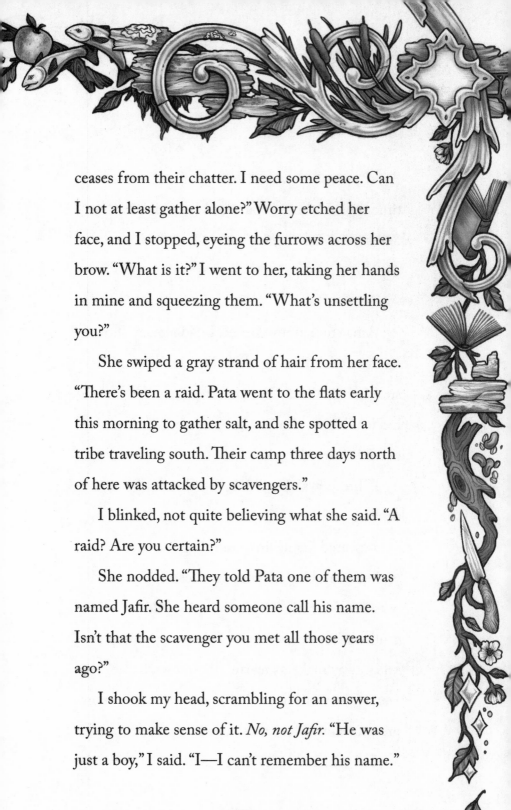

ceases from their chatter. I need some peace. Can
I not at least gather alone?" Worry etched her
face, and I stopped, eyeing the furrows across her
brow. "What is it?" I went to her, taking her hands
in mine and squeezing them. "What's unsettling
you?"

She swiped a gray strand of hair from her face.
"There's been a raid. Pata went to the flats early
this morning to gather salt, and she spotted a
tribe traveling south. Their camp three days north
of here was attacked by scavengers."

I blinked, not quite believing what she said. "A
raid? Are you certain?"

She nodded. "They told Pata one of them was
named Jafir. She heard someone call his name.
Isn't that the scavenger you met all those years
ago?"

I shook my head, scrambling for an answer,
trying to make sense of it. *No, not Jafir.* "He was
just a boy," I said. "I—I can't remember his name."

Every part of me was dazed, numb. "It was a long time ago." My mind spun, and I couldn't focus. *Scavengers? Jafir raiding a camp?*

No.

No.

Ama studied my silence. I had already shown her too much fear. I gathered my doubts and steadied my voice. "We are safe, Ama. We are hidden. No one knows we are here, and three days north is a very long way."

"Three days of walking, yes. But not for scavengers on swift horses."

I assured her again, reminding her how long we had been here without ever seeing anyone outside of our tribe. I promised I would be cautious, but said we couldn't let one sighting miles away make us fearful of our own home. *Home.* The word floated in my chest, feeling more precious now. More threatened.

She reluctantly let me go, and I hurried down

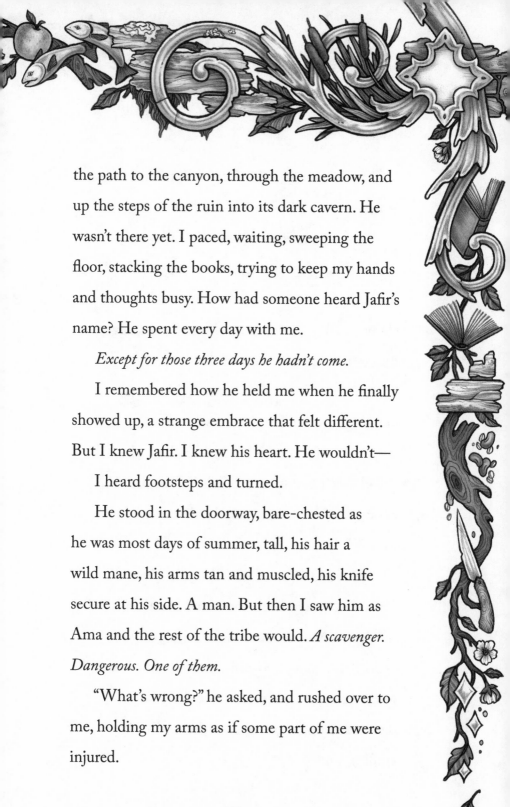

the path to the canyon, through the meadow, and up the steps of the ruin into its dark cavern. He wasn't there yet. I paced, waiting, sweeping the floor, stacking the books, trying to keep my hands and thoughts busy. How had someone heard Jafir's name? He spent every day with me.

Except for those three days he hadn't come.

I remembered how he held me when he finally showed up, a strange embrace that felt different. But I knew Jafir. I knew his heart. He wouldn't—

I heard footsteps and turned.

He stood in the doorway, bare-chested as he was most days of summer, tall, his hair a wild mane, his arms tan and muscled, his knife secure at his side. A man. But then I saw him as Ama and the rest of the tribe would. *A scavenger. Dangerous. One of them.*

"What's wrong?" he asked, and rushed over to me, holding my arms as if some part of me were injured.

"There's been a raid. A tribe in the north was attacked."

I saw all I needed to know in his eyes. I pulled free, sobs jumping to my throat. "By the gods, Jafir." I stumbled away, unable to see clearly, wishing I were anywhere else. I staggered deeper into the darkness of the ruin.

"Let me explain," he begged, following, grabbing my hand, trying to stop me.

I jerked free and whirled. "Explain what?" I yelled. "What did you get, Jafir? Their bread? A baby goat? What did you take that didn't belong to you?"

He stared at me, a vein rising in his neck. His chest rose in deep, measured breaths. "I had no choice, Morrighan. I had to ride with my clan. That is how I got this," he said, motioning to the fading bruise on his face. "My father demanded that I go. Our northern kin were coming, and—"

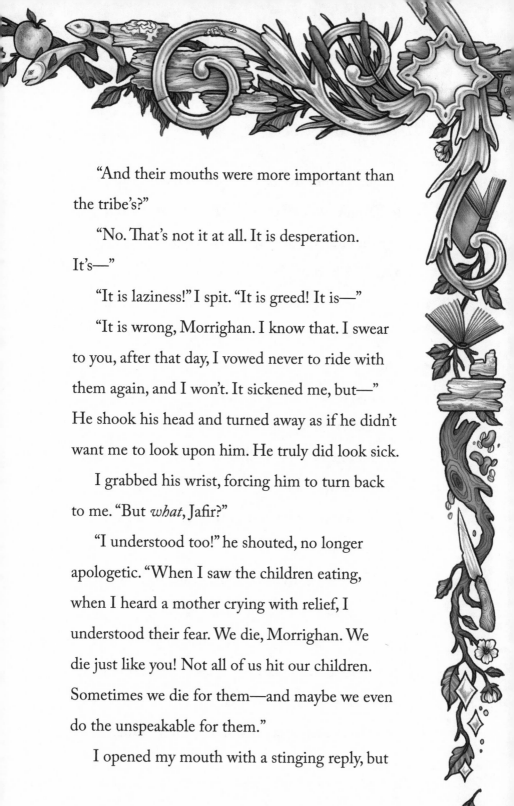

"And their mouths were more important than the tribe's?"

"No. That's not it at all. It is desperation. It's—"

"It is laziness!" I spit. "It is greed! It is—"

"It is wrong, Morrighan. I know that. I swear to you, after that day, I vowed never to ride with them again, and I won't. It sickened me, but—" He shook his head and turned away as if he didn't want me to look upon him. He truly did look sick.

I grabbed his wrist, forcing him to turn back to me. "But *what*, Jafir?"

"I understood too!" he shouted, no longer apologetic. "When I saw the children eating, when I heard a mother crying with relief, I understood their fear. We die, Morrighan. We die just like you! Not all of us hit our children. Sometimes we die for them—and maybe we even do the unspeakable for them."

I opened my mouth with a stinging reply, but

the anguish in his expression made me swallow it. Fatigue washed over me. I stared at the floor, my shoulders suddenly heavy. "How many?" I asked. "Children?"

"Eight." His voice was as thin as mist. "The oldest is seven, the youngest only a few months old."

I squeezed my eyes shut. *It was still no excuse!*

"Morrighan. Please."

I looked up. He pulled me to his chest, and my tears were warm against his shoulder. "I'm sorry," he whispered into my hair. "I promise it won't happen again."

"You're a scavenger, Jafir," I said, feeling the hopelessness of who he was.

"But I want to be more. I will be more." He lifted my face to his, kissing away a tear on my cheek, his own eyes wet with grief.

"So . . . *this* is what you've been hunting every day."

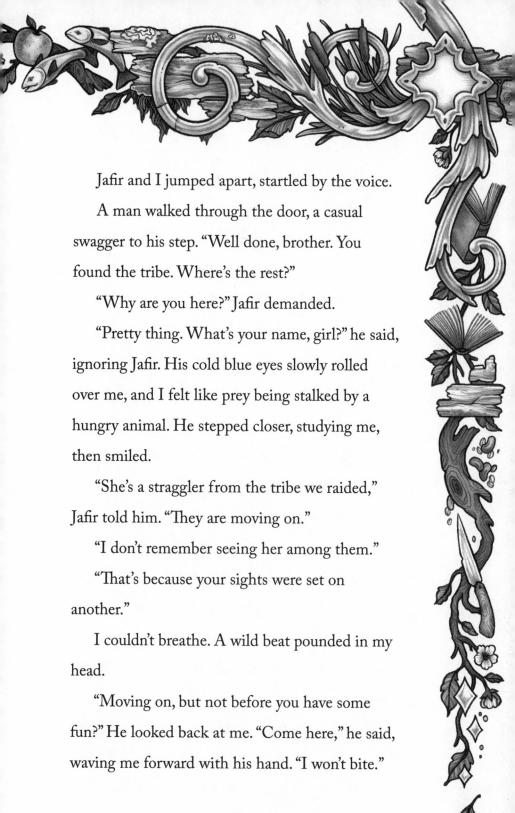

Jafir and I jumped apart, startled by the voice.

A man walked through the door, a casual swagger to his step. "Well done, brother. You found the tribe. Where's the rest?"

"Why are you here?" Jafir demanded.

"Pretty thing. What's your name, girl?" he said, ignoring Jafir. His cold blue eyes slowly rolled over me, and I felt like prey being stalked by a hungry animal. He stepped closer, studying me, then smiled.

"She's a straggler from the tribe we raided," Jafir told him. "They are moving on."

"I don't remember seeing her among them."

"That's because your sights were set on another."

I couldn't breathe. A wild beat pounded in my head.

"Moving on, but not before you have some fun?" He looked back at me. "Come here," he said, waving me forward with his hand. "I won't bite."

Jafir stepped in front of me. "What do you want, Steffan?"

"Just what you've been enjoying. We are kin. We share." He moved to step around Jafir, and Jafir lunged at him. They both stumbled back and slammed up against the far wall. Dust rained down around them. Though Jafir was taller, Steffan was stout, built more like a bull, and there was weight behind his fist. He grunted as he punched Jafir in the gut, then again in the jaw. Jafir staggered back, stunned for only a moment before he swung, his fist cracking against his brother's chin. He didn't let up and lunged again, knocking Steffan to the floor, and in an instant, Jafir was holding a knife to his brother's throat.

"Go ahead," Jafir yelled. "Make a move! I'd love to slash your thick neck once and for all!" He pressed the blade closer.

Steffan glared at me, then back at his brother. "You are greedy, Jafir. Keep her to yourself, then,"

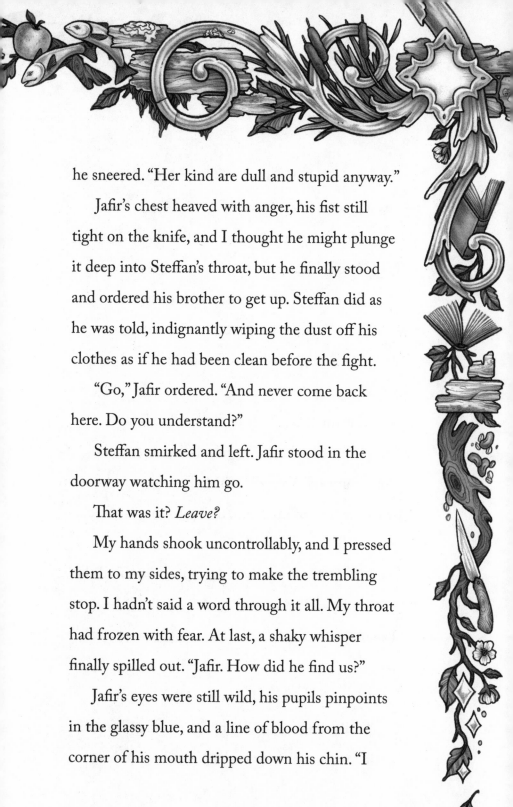

he sneered. "Her kind are dull and stupid anyway."

Jafir's chest heaved with anger, his fist still tight on the knife, and I thought he might plunge it deep into Steffan's throat, but he finally stood and ordered his brother to get up. Steffan did as he was told, indignantly wiping the dust off his clothes as if he had been clean before the fight.

"Go," Jafir ordered. "And never come back here. Do you understand?"

Steffan smirked and left. Jafir stood in the doorway watching him go.

That was it? *Leave?*

My hands shook uncontrollably, and I pressed them to my sides, trying to make the trembling stop. I hadn't said a word through it all. My throat had frozen with fear. At last, a shaky whisper finally spilled out. "Jafir. How did he find us?"

Jafir's eyes were still wild, his pupils pinpoints in the glassy blue, and a line of blood from the corner of his mouth dripped down his chin. "I

don't know. He must have followed me. I was always careful, but today—"

"What are we going to do?" I sobbed. "He'll come back! I know he will!"

Jafir grabbed my hands, trying to stop the shaking. "Yes, he will come back, which means you never can, Morrighan. Ever. We'll find another place for us—"

"But the tribe! They're not far! He'll find them! How could you let him follow you, Jafir? You promised! You—" I whirled, wiping my brow with the heel of my hand, trying to think, panic rising in me.

Jafir grabbed my shoulders. "He *won't* find the tribe. You said yourself the vale is well hidden. I've never found it. Steffan is lazy. He won't even try."

"But what if he tells the others?"

"Tells them what? That he found a girl from a tribe we had already raided? A tribe that had

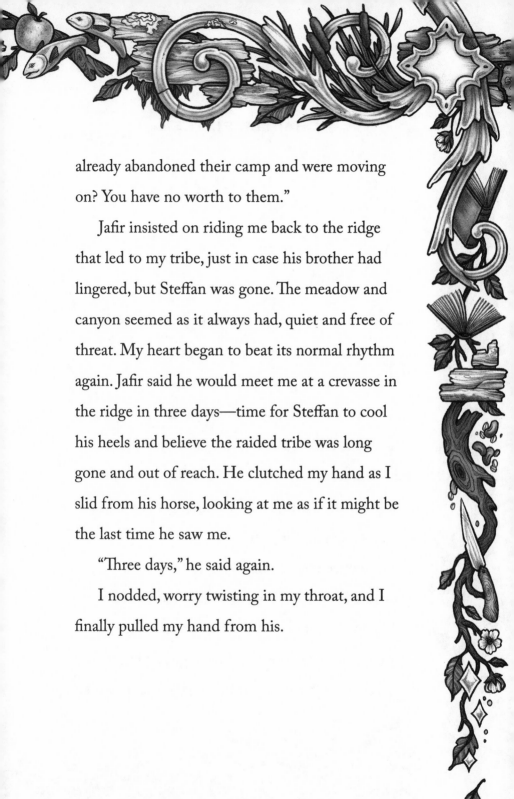

already abandoned their camp and were moving
on? You have no worth to them."

Jafir insisted on riding me back to the ridge
that led to my tribe, just in case his brother had
lingered, but Steffan was gone. The meadow and
canyon seemed as it always had, quiet and free of
threat. My heart began to beat its normal rhythm
again. Jafir said he would meet me at a crevasse in
the ridge in three days—time for Steffan to cool
his heels and believe the raided tribe was long
gone and out of reach. He clutched my hand as I
slid from his horse, looking at me as if it might be
the last time he saw me.

"Three days," he said again.

I nodded, worry twisting in my throat, and I
finally pulled my hand from his.

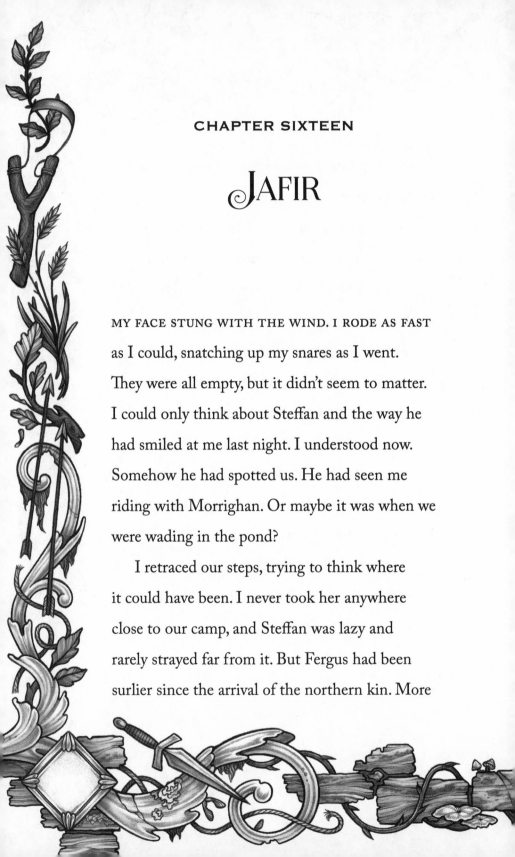

CHAPTER SIXTEEN

JAFIR

MY FACE STUNG WITH THE WIND. I RODE AS FAST as I could, snatching up my snares as I went. They were all empty, but it didn't seem to matter. I could only think about Steffan and the way he had smiled at me last night. I understood now. Somehow he had spotted us. He had seen me riding with Morrighan. Or maybe it was when we were wading in the pond?

I retraced our steps, trying to think where it could have been. I never took her anywhere close to our camp, and Steffan was lazy and rarely strayed far from it. But Fergus had been surlier since the arrival of the northern kin. More insistent on building up our stores. No one was to come back empty-handed, and—now it struck me with clarity—of course Steffan would follow on my heels, since I was the better hunter. Maybe it was he who had already emptied my snares.

The sight of him coming upon Morrighan and me flashed through my mind again, standing in the doorway, composed and confident. That same smug smile as the evening before had been smeared across his face.

Dread prickled across my shoulders, and my hands tightened on the reins. *How long had he been standing there listening?* The dread ignited to burning fear. *Morrighan.* I tried to remember every word I'd said, but it was all a jumble—me trying to convince her I would never raid a tribe again, the despair in her eyes, the disappointment, my promises. *But did I say her name?* Did he hear me call her Morrighan?

What's your name, girl? he had asked.

Why would Steffan care about a name unless he suspected? Unless he'd heard. He hadn't asked the girl from the other tribe her name.

But the name Morrighan had great worth—at least to one person—which made it valuable to Steffan too.

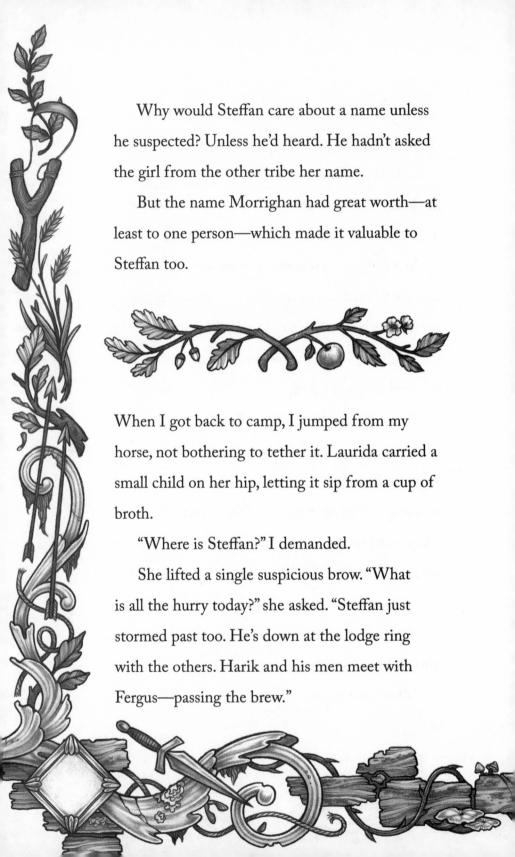

When I got back to camp, I jumped from my horse, not bothering to tether it. Laurida carried a small child on her hip, letting it sip from a cup of broth.

"Where is Steffan?" I demanded.

She lifted a single suspicious brow. "What is all the hurry today?" she asked. "Steffan just stormed past too. He's down at the lodge ring with the others. Harik and his men meet with Fergus—passing the brew."

Sweat sprang to my face. *No, not Harik. Not today.* I ran to the lodge, but it was already too late. Steffan was strutting around the cold fire ring, announcing his find to them all—a girl of the tribespeople.

"I found her," he said. "Morrighan."

The group fell silent. Harik's features sharpened, and he leaned forward. Of course Steffan didn't mention me—the find had to be all his. He basked in the attention of Harik and Fergus, telling them the story of his cunning stealth.

I glared at him. "How would you know it's her?"

"She was talking to a foolish little maiden who squeaked her name."

When Fergus asked why he hadn't brought her there, Steffan claimed he was on his horse on a ridge high above them, and when the girls spotted him, they ran. But he saw the direction

they headed. The camp was near. I was almost in awe at how quickly he conjured stories. I knew it was not to protect me but to keep the glory—and the likely reward—to himself.

Harik took a long sip of his brew. "Then that means the old woman is near too. So many years . . ." He said it more to himself than to us. His voice was thick with curiosity. "Their supplies are probably great." But his interest seemed to be in more than just their stores of food.

They began to make plans to ride to the camp, but Steffan quickly backtracked, saying he hadn't seen exactly where it was. "But I can lead us close enough. At night they will surely have a fire to help us find them."

I stepped forward, scoffing at Steffan's claim. "I saw the tribe we raided a few days ago just east of here and heading south," I said. "She was probably one of them. Why waste our time?"

Steffan insisted she wasn't one of them, and

the more I argued that we shouldn't go, the angrier he got—the angrier everyone got, except Harik. He regarded me with a cool eye, his chin lifting slightly. Everyone noticed and quieted.

"Let the boy stay behind if that's what he wants," he said as he stood. "But he'll enjoy none of the fruits of our ride." He looked at Fergus for confirmation.

Fergus glared at me. I had humiliated him in front of Harik. "None," he confirmed.

They all moved toward their horses—our men plus Harik and his four. I couldn't stop them all. I had to go along.

"I'm coming," I said, already trying to think of ways I could lead them astray. And if I couldn't do that and they should find the camp, I knew I had to keep myself between Steffan and Morrighan.

CHAPTER SEVENTEEN

MORRIGHAN

JAFIR AND I HAD HAD A LIFETIME BETWEEN US. There seemed to be no before—not one that mattered. My days were measured not in hours but by the flecks of bright color that danced in his eyes as he looked into mine, by the sun on our hands laced together, our shoulders touching as we read, by his laughter when I teased him. His smile came easily now. The scowling, skinny boy had become a distant, hazy memory. *His smile.* My stomach twisted.

We had something that was too long and lasting to be wiped away in a single day—or by a mistake. He was not like the others. *Come*

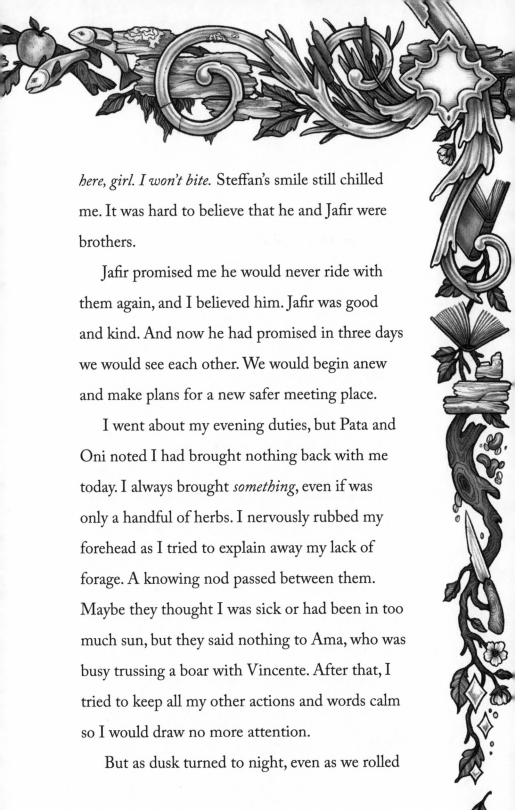

here, girl. I won't bite. Steffan's smile still chilled me. It was hard to believe that he and Jafir were brothers.

Jafir promised me he would never ride with them again, and I believed him. Jafir was good and kind. And now he had promised in three days we would see each other. We would begin anew and make plans for a new safer meeting place.

I went about my evening duties, but Pata and Oni noted I had brought nothing back with me today. I always brought *something*, even if was only a handful of herbs. I nervously rubbed my forehead as I tried to explain away my lack of forage. A knowing nod passed between them. Maybe they thought I was sick or had been in too much sun, but they said nothing to Ama, who was busy trussing a boar with Vincente. After that, I tried to keep all my other actions and words calm so I would draw no more attention.

But as dusk turned to night, even as we rolled

back the skins to let a breeze pass through the longhouse, even as I ground herbs to powder, even as I added twigs and branches to the fire to keep the boar roasting, I knew. Jafir and I would not meet at the crevasse in three days. We would not meet there ever.

> *It is in the sorrows.*
> *In the fear.*
> *In the need.*
> *That is when the knowing gains wings.*

Ama had used many different ways to explain it to me. *When the few who were left had nothing else, they had to return to the way of knowing. It is how they survived.*

But this knowing that crouched in my gut felt nothing like wings.

Instead, it was something dark and heavy, squeezing each knot of my spine one at a time, like steps getting closer. Those few days would

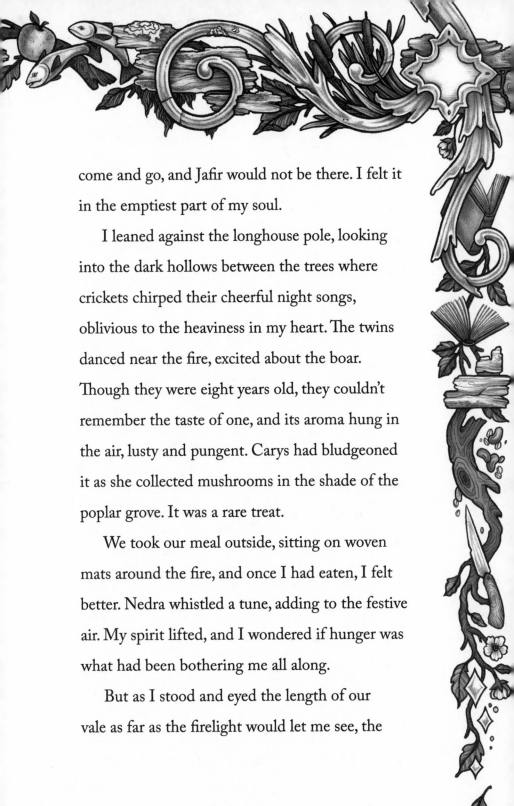

come and go, and Jafir would not be there. I felt it in the emptiest part of my soul.

I leaned against the longhouse pole, looking into the dark hollows between the trees where crickets chirped their cheerful night songs, oblivious to the heaviness in my heart. The twins danced near the fire, excited about the boar. Though they were eight years old, they couldn't remember the taste of one, and its aroma hung in the air, lusty and pungent. Carys had bludgeoned it as she collected mushrooms in the shade of the poplar grove. It was a rare treat.

We took our meal outside, sitting on woven mats around the fire, and once I had eaten, I felt better. Nedra whistled a tune, adding to the festive air. My spirit lifted, and I wondered if hunger was what had been bothering me all along.

But as I stood and eyed the length of our vale as far as the firelight would let me see, the

heaviness gripped me again, squeezing away my breath. It made no sense. There was nothing but peace, but then Ama came up behind me and laid a hand on my shoulder.

"What are you feeling?" she asked.

I saw it in her eyes too.

"Let's douse the fire," she said, "and get the children and others inside." But it was already too late.

The sound was sudden, roaring down upon us, the pounding of hooves that seemed to come from all sides. There was confusion at first— the twins screaming, everyone turning, trying to see what it was—and then they were there, the scavengers surrounding us, circling on their horses, making sure none of us ran. They were a skilled pack of wolves, and we were their prey. And then I heard the voice, the one Ama hates. He was leading them. *Harik.* The tribe remained frozen and quiet. Rhiann's death was still fresh

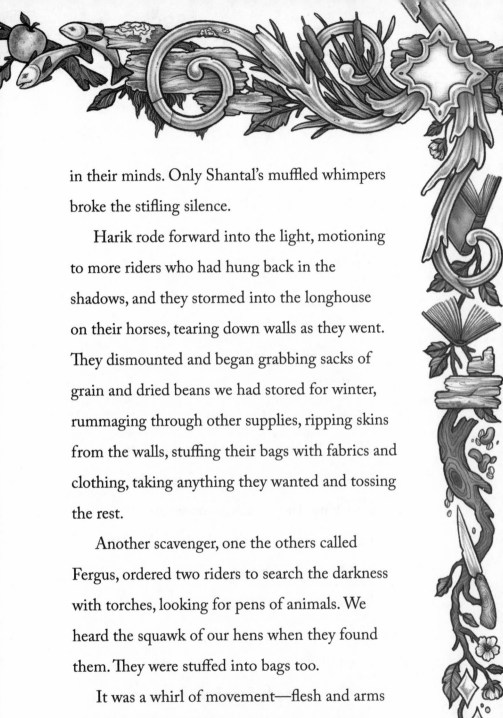

in their minds. Only Shantal's muffled whimpers broke the stifling silence.

Harik rode forward into the light, motioning to more riders who had hung back in the shadows, and they stormed into the longhouse on their horses, tearing down walls as they went. They dismounted and began grabbing sacks of grain and dried beans we had stored for winter, rummaging through other supplies, ripping skins from the walls, stuffing their bags with fabrics and clothing, taking anything they wanted and tossing the rest.

Another scavenger, one the others called Fergus, ordered two riders to search the darkness with torches, looking for pens of animals. We heard the squawk of our hens when they found them. They were stuffed into bags too.

It was a whirl of movement—flesh and arms and fervor—making it hard to distinguish one scavenger from another in their careless zeal. But

then there was a color. A flash. A cheekbone. A
chest. A long cord of golden hair.

The clamor was suddenly distorted, muted,
the world slowing. Tumbling upside down.

Jafir.

Jafir rode with them.

He hoisted a large bag of grain onto the
back of his horse.

My bones turned to water.

He had led them here. He worked side
by side with his brother. They were skilled
at ransacking. They showed no mercy or
compassion. It was over quickly, and they left
the longhouse to circle around us.

Jafir's eyes met mine, and my numbness
vanished.

I trembled with rage. Steffan reached for
what little remained of the boar still on the spit
and set about wrapping it in a skin to take too.
I spotted the knife Carys had used to cut the

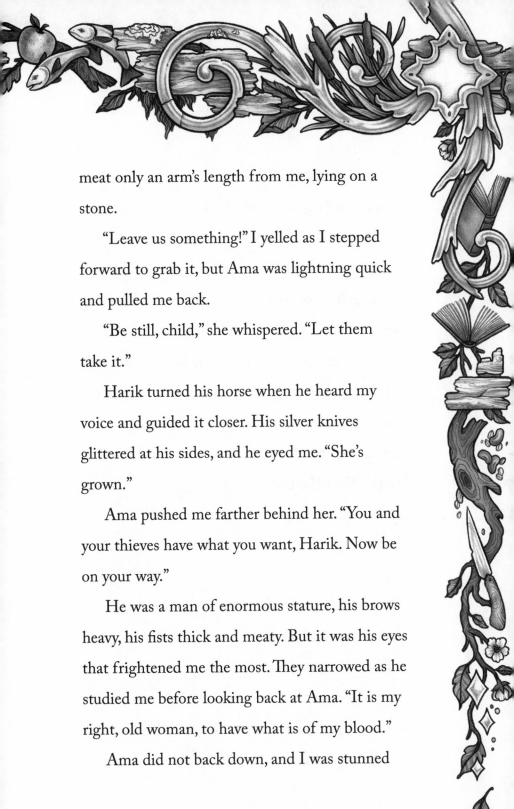

meat only an arm's length from me, lying on a stone.

"Leave us something!" I yelled as I stepped forward to grab it, but Ama was lightning quick and pulled me back.

"Be still, child," she whispered. "Let them take it."

Harik turned his horse when he heard my voice and guided it closer. His silver knives glittered at his sides, and he eyed me. "She's grown."

Ama pushed me farther behind her. "You and your thieves have what you want, Harik. Now be on your way."

He was a man of enormous stature, his brows heavy, his fists thick and meaty. But it was his eyes that frightened me the most. They narrowed as he studied me before looking back at Ama. "It is my right, old woman, to have what is of my blood."

Ama did not back down, and I was stunned

at their familiarity with each other. "You have no rights here," she said. "She is nothing of yours."

"So you'd like to believe," he said. His gaze turned back to me. "Look at her hair. The fierce gleam in her eye. She wants to kill us all. That is mine." I could not mistake the pride in his voice. My stomach turned over, and my head ached. I felt my meal rise in my throat, the boar alive and gamey. My memory flashed with the whispers of Ama, Oni, and Nedra, the whispers that I had long denied. The truth.

I swallowed my disgust and shouted, "You are nothing but an animal to me, the same as the others."

Steffan bolted toward me, spouting about lessons and my lack of respect, but Jafir stepped in front of him, knocking him to the side and advancing toward me in his place. He raised his arm, the back of his hand poised to strike me. "Hold your tongue, girl, unless you'd like me to

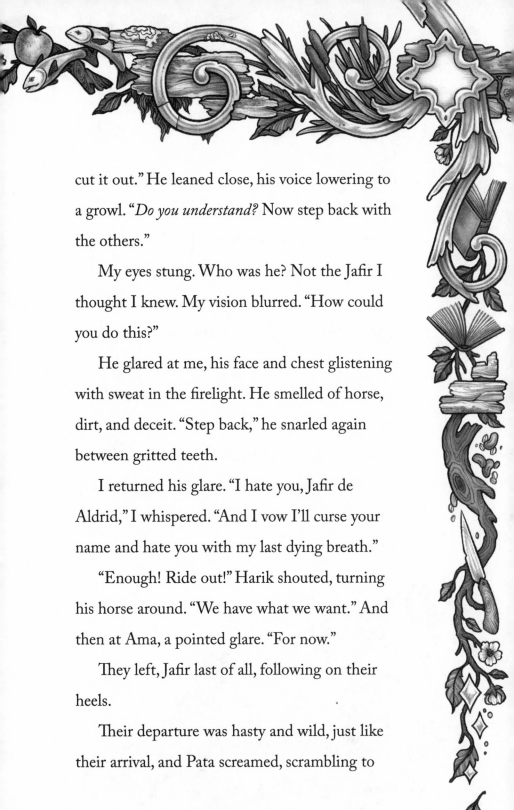

cut it out." He leaned close, his voice lowering to a growl. "*Do you understand?* Now step back with the others."

My eyes stung. Who was he? Not the Jafir I thought I knew. My vision blurred. "How could you do this?"

He glared at me, his face and chest glistening with sweat in the firelight. He smelled of horse, dirt, and deceit. "Step back," he snarled again between gritted teeth.

I returned his glare. "I hate you, Jafir de Aldrid," I whispered. "And I vow I'll curse your name and hate you with my last dying breath."

"Enough! Ride out!" Harik shouted, turning his horse around. "We have what we want." And then at Ama, a pointed glare. "For now."

They left, Jafir last of all, following on their heels.

Their departure was hasty and wild, just like their arrival, and Pata screamed, scrambling to

avoid a horse charging in her direction. She

fell, but the horses kept going. One stepped

on her, crushing her leg. She writhed in pain,

and we ran to her aid. Carys felt through the

fabric of Pata's trousers and winced. "It is badly

broken." The turmoil of the raid was temporarily

forgotten as we focused on Pata. Six of us

carefully lifted and carried her to what was left

of the longhouse and cleared a place among the

scattered debris to lay her down. Carys gently

cut away the fabric of Pata's trousers to examine

her leg as Oni whispered words of comfort into

her ear.

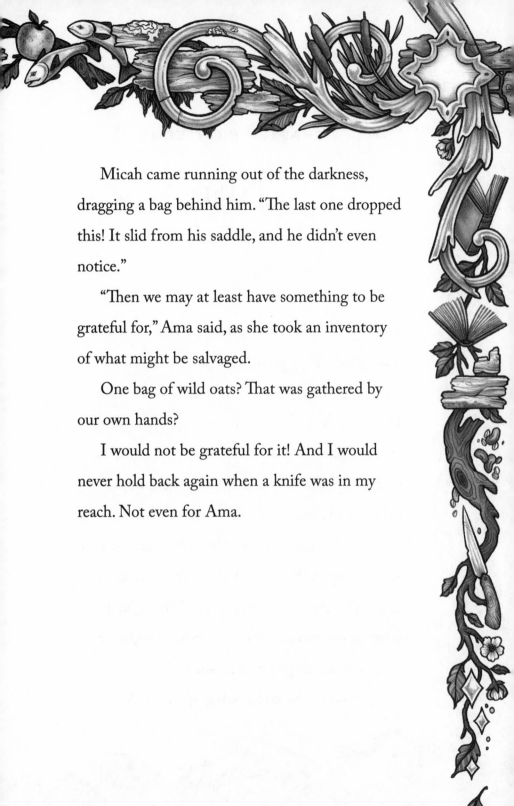

Micah came running out of the darkness, dragging a bag behind him. "The last one dropped this! It slid from his saddle, and he didn't even notice."

"Then we may at least have something to be grateful for," Ama said, as she took an inventory of what might be salvaged.

One bag of wild oats? That was gathered by our own hands?

I would not be grateful for it! And I would never hold back again when a knife was in my reach. Not even for Ama.

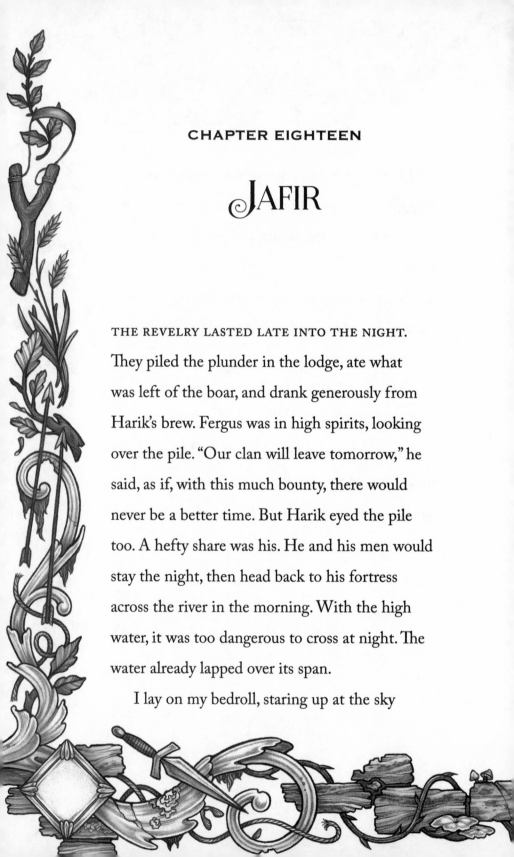

CHAPTER EIGHTEEN

JAFIR

THE REVELRY LASTED LATE INTO THE NIGHT.
They piled the plunder in the lodge, ate what
was left of the boar, and drank generously from
Harik's brew. Fergus was in high spirits, looking
over the pile. "Our clan will leave tomorrow," he
said, as if, with this much bounty, there would
never be a better time. But Harik eyed the pile
too. A hefty share was his. He and his men would
stay the night, then head back to his fortress
across the river in the morning. With the high
water, it was too dangerous to cross at night. The
water already lapped over its span.

I lay on my bedroll, staring up at the sky

between the open rafters. My arms and legs twitched with exhaustion. Every part of me had been tight and ready to pounce for hours. I'd done everything I could to lead them astray, even saying I had spotted fires in opposite directions. But when the strong smell of roasting boar wafted across our trail, there was no stopping them.

My muscles had coiled into knots as I watched Harik and Steffan, uncertain what they would do. Uncertain what any of them would do.

And then seeing Morrighan. Her eyes. Her expression.

I hate you, Jafir . . . I will hate you with my last dying breath.

And she should. I closed my eyes.

We were leaving. She'd be grateful for that. She would never have to see me again.

But I would always see her. Until I drew my last breath, it would always be her face I saw when I closed my eyes at night, and her face again

when I woke each morning. I would force myself
to forget the last words I heard from her lips. I
would remember others.

I love you, Jafir de Aldrid. Words that, now, I
was sure I had never deserved.

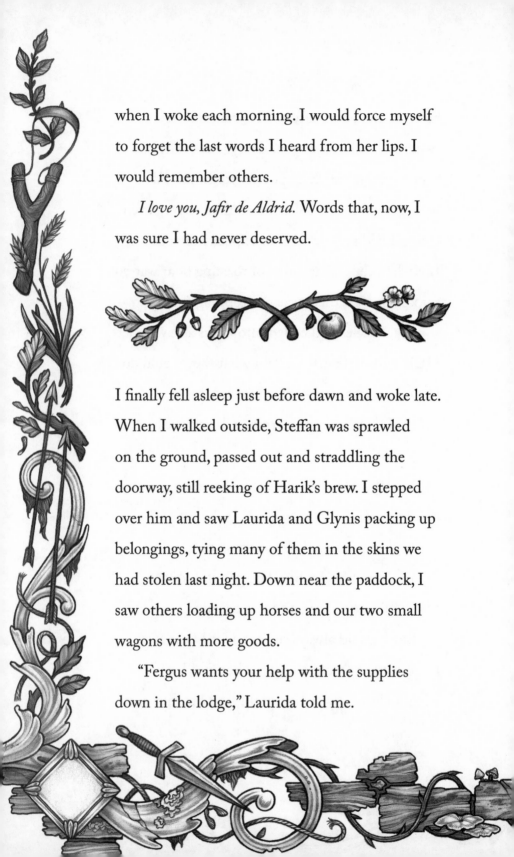

I finally fell asleep just before dawn and woke late.
When I walked outside, Steffan was sprawled
on the ground, passed out and straddling the
doorway, still reeking of Harik's brew. I stepped
over him and saw Laurida and Glynis packing up
belongings, tying many of them in the skins we
had stolen last night. Down near the paddock, I
saw others loading up horses and our two small
wagons with more goods.

"Fergus wants your help with the supplies
down in the lodge," Laurida told me.

When I got there, he was alone, putting the supplies into stacks. "Where are Harik and his men?" I asked.

"Gone." Fergus didn't look up, still consumed with the goods, his eyes heavy from little sleep.

I looked at the supplies. They were all still there. "Harik didn't take his share?"

"His gift to us. I think he was reluctant to leave it behind, but the girl was on his mind more than the supplies. She was enough. He thanked us for finding her."

I was groggy from lack of sleep and thought I had missed something. "What do you mean, *the girl was enough?*"

"He thinks she has the knowing, like her grandmother. He went to get her before he crosses the bridge."

"He's taking her? Now?"

"It's his right. She's—"

"No!" I shook my head, turning in all

139

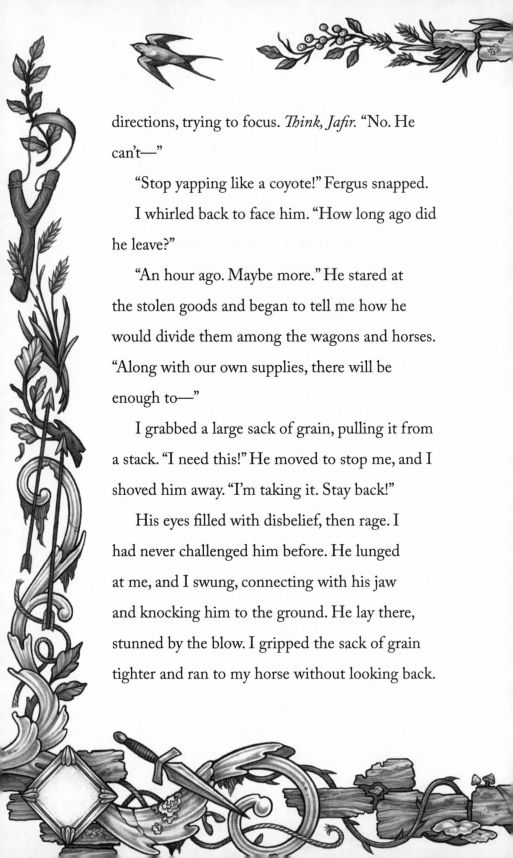

directions, trying to focus. *Think, Jafir.* "No. He can't—"

"Stop yapping like a coyote!" Fergus snapped.

I whirled back to face him. "How long ago did he leave?"

"An hour ago. Maybe more." He stared at the stolen goods and began to tell me how he would divide them among the wagons and horses. "Along with our own supplies, there will be enough to—"

I grabbed a large sack of grain, pulling it from a stack. "I need this!" He moved to stop me, and I shoved him away. "I'm taking it. Stay back!"

His eyes filled with disbelief, then rage. I had never challenged him before. He lunged at me, and I swung, connecting with his jaw and knocking him to the ground. He lay there, stunned by the blow. I gripped the sack of grain tighter and ran to my horse without looking back.

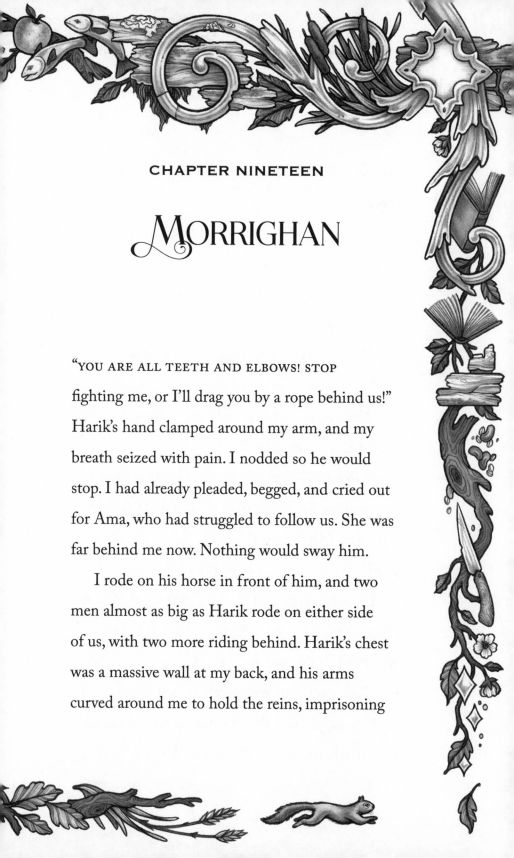

CHAPTER NINETEEN

MORRIGHAN

"YOU ARE ALL TEETH AND ELBOWS! STOP
fighting me, or I'll drag you by a rope behind us!"
Harik's hand clamped around my arm, and my
breath seized with pain. I nodded so he would
stop. I had already pleaded, begged, and cried out
for Ama, who had struggled to follow us. She was
far behind me now. Nothing would sway him.

I rode on his horse in front of him, and two
men almost as big as Harik rode on either side
of us, with two more riding behind. Harik's chest
was a massive wall at my back, and his arms
curved around me to hold the reins, imprisoning

me like a shackle. Sobs still jumped from my throat.

"And stop that noise!" he ordered. "I am your father!"

"You are no father of mine," I seethed. "You are nothing!"

"The old woman has poisoned you against me."

"No poison was required. You've earned my hatred all on your own."

"Morrighan," he said, not to me, but to the air. He grumbled a low sigh, as if the name brought him grief. "She chose that name long before you were born. I cared for your mother."

I squeezed my eyes shut. I didn't want to hear about my mother from him. I spit to the side, wishing I could turn and hit his face instead. "You cared so much that you stole my aunt too?"

"I stole neither. Venda came on her own, and your mother never left the tribe. She met with

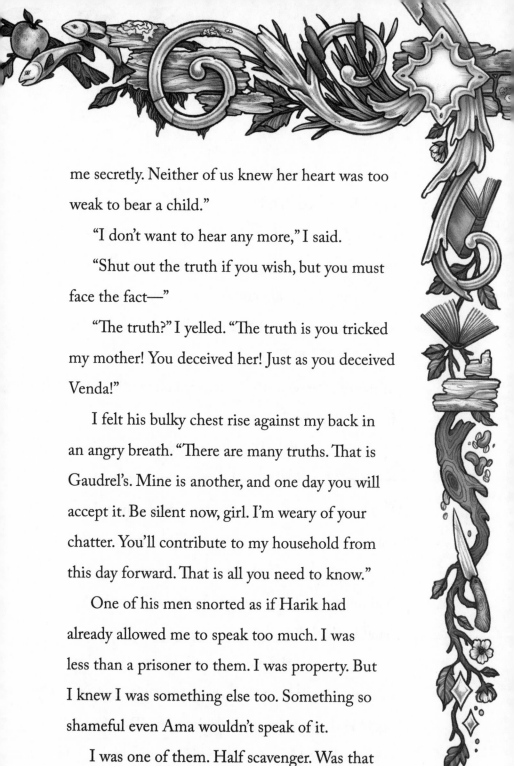

me secretly. Neither of us knew her heart was too weak to bear a child."

"I don't want to hear any more," I said.

"Shut out the truth if you wish, but you must face the fact—"

"The truth?" I yelled. "The truth is you tricked my mother! You deceived her! Just as you deceived Venda!"

I felt his bulky chest rise against my back in an angry breath. "There are many truths. That is Gaudrel's. Mine is another, and one day you will accept it. Be silent now, girl. I'm weary of your chatter. You'll contribute to my household from this day forward. That is all you need to know."

One of his men snorted as if Harik had already allowed me to speak too much. I was less than a prisoner to them. I was property. But I knew I was something else too. Something so shameful even Ama wouldn't speak of it.

I was one of them. Half scavenger. Was that

why she had lied about my father being dead?
Had she hoped that by erasing it from memory,
it would erase the truth? Was there some part of
me—his part—always in danger of coming to
the surface? My skin crawled thinking of it, and I
wished I could banish the knowledge of him from
my head. The hideous ruins on the other side
of the river grew in the distance, along with the
fortress that would soon be my home.

I thought of my last glimpse of Ama reaching
out for me, and tears welled in my eyes again. We
had been making a pallet to carry Pata when they
came. In another hour, we would have been gone,
but no one had expected a return visit so soon. We
had nothing left for them to take—at least that's
what we had thought.

As we rode, the memory of Jafir emerging out
of the darkness with the other scavengers flashed
again and again through my thoughts. The chaotic
events whirled in contrast to his strained and

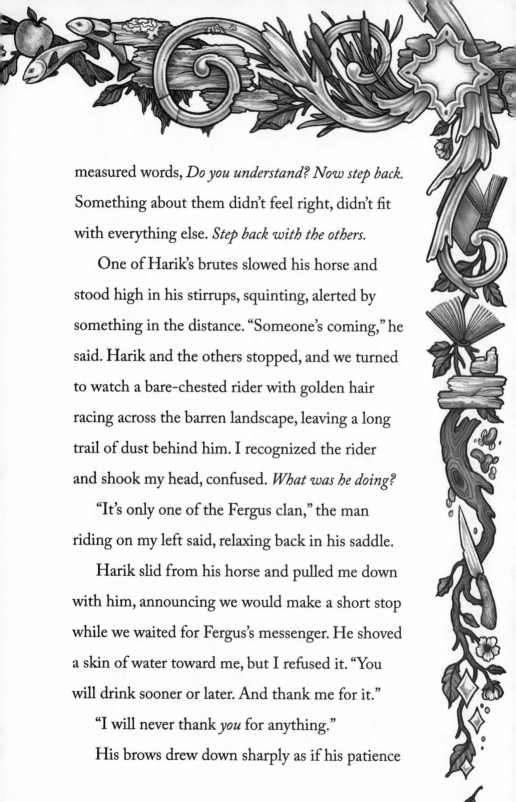

measured words, *Do you understand? Now step back.*
Something about them didn't feel right, didn't fit
with everything else. *Step back with the others.*

One of Harik's brutes slowed his horse and
stood high in his stirrups, squinting, alerted by
something in the distance. "Someone's coming," he
said. Harik and the others stopped, and we turned
to watch a bare-chested rider with golden hair
racing across the barren landscape, leaving a long
trail of dust behind him. I recognized the rider
and shook my head, confused. *What was he doing?*

"It's only one of the Fergus clan," the man
riding on my left said, relaxing back in his saddle.

Harik slid from his horse and pulled me down
with him, announcing we would make a short stop
while we waited for Fergus's messenger. He shoved
a skin of water toward me, but I refused it. "You
will drink sooner or later. And thank me for it."

"I will never thank *you* for anything."

His brows drew down sharply as if his patience

was spent, and I thought he might strike me—but then he paused, studying me—and something else passed through his eyes. He shook his head and looked away. I wondered if he had seen some part of my mother when he studied me. Ama said I looked just like her except for my hair. My dark, wavy locks were like Harik's. *I cared for your mother. She met me secretly.* Lies. All lies.

The wild thud of hooves descended on us, and Jafir pulled back, bringing his horse to a quick stop. He jumped from his saddle but avoided my gaze, looking only at Harik. He wasted no time letting him know the purpose of his visit. "I've come to make a trade. I have a bag of grain for you in exchange for her."

Harik stared at him, then finally laughed, realizing Jafir was serious. "A single bag of grain? For her? She's far more valuable than that."

Jafir's eyes turned molten. "It is all I have. You will take it."

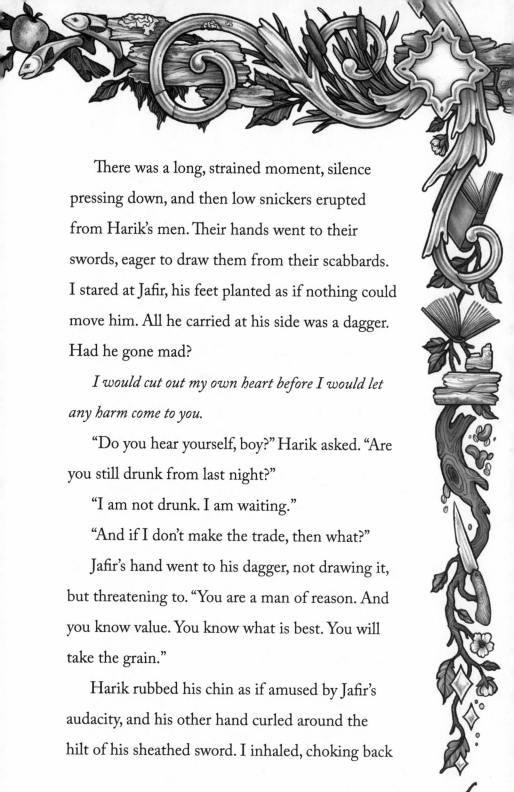

There was a long, strained moment, silence
pressing down, and then low snickers erupted
from Harik's men. Their hands went to their
swords, eager to draw them from their scabbards.
I stared at Jafir, his feet planted as if nothing could
move him. All he carried at his side was a dagger.
Had he gone mad?

*I would cut out my own heart before I would let
any harm come to you.*

"Do you hear yourself, boy?" Harik asked. "Are
you still drunk from last night?"

"I am not drunk. I am waiting."

"And if I don't make the trade, then what?"

Jafir's hand went to his dagger, not drawing it,
but threatening to. "You are a man of reason. And
you know value. You know what is best. You will
take the grain."

Harik rubbed his chin as if amused by Jafir's
audacity, and his other hand curled around the
hilt of his sheathed sword. I inhaled, choking back

a moan. Harik's gaze shot to me, and our eyes locked. I couldn't breathe. He scrutinized me, his gaze cutting straight into my skull, his expression impossible to read, and then he finally grunted, shaking his head. "So that's how it is."

He turned back to Jafir, a deep line furrowing across his brow in a scowl. "You are a fool, boy. I am getting the better deal. She is trouble, this one. But have it your way! Take her!" He shoved me toward Jafir, and I stumbled, almost falling. Once I got my footing, I looked back at Harik uncertainly, wondering if it was a trick.

His gaze softened and his eyes lingered on me a moment longer as if he wanted to say something else, but then he turned abruptly to his men and yelled, "The deal is made! Take the grain from his horse, and let's go!"

In seconds they were gone. I watched them ride off, galloping toward the bridge.

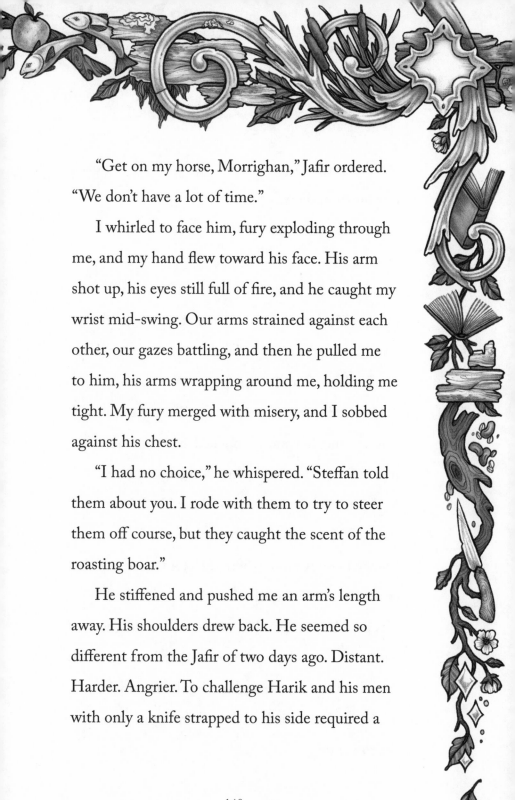

"Get on my horse, Morrighan," Jafir ordered.
"We don't have a lot of time."

I whirled to face him, fury exploding through
me, and my hand flew toward his face. His arm
shot up, his eyes still full of fire, and he caught my
wrist mid-swing. Our arms strained against each
other, our gazes battling, and then he pulled me
to him, his arms wrapping around me, holding me
tight. My fury merged with misery, and I sobbed
against his chest.

"I had no choice," he whispered. "Steffan told
them about you. I rode with them to try to steer
them off course, but they caught the scent of the
roasting boar."

He stiffened and pushed me an arm's length
away. His shoulders drew back. He seemed so
different from the Jafir of two days ago. Distant.
Harder. Angrier. To challenge Harik and his men
with only a knife strapped to his side required a

certain amount of savage lunacy. "I'll take you back to your camp now."

"So you're not *buying* me with my own sack of grain?"

His nostrils flared. "Go ahead. Be angry. Hate me. You'll never have to see me after today. That should make you happy. I'm leaving with my clan. They still need me."

I stared at him. *Never.* A familiar ache wormed through me. My mouth opened, but no words would form. "You're leaving," I finally repeated.

"This can't be all there is," he said. "It is no way to live. There has to be a better place than this. Somewhere. A place where the children in my clan can have a different life than the one I've had." His jaw clenched, and he added with a rougher edge, "A place where someone can fall in love with whoever they choose and not be shamed by it."

He grabbed his horse's lead and motioned for me to get up.

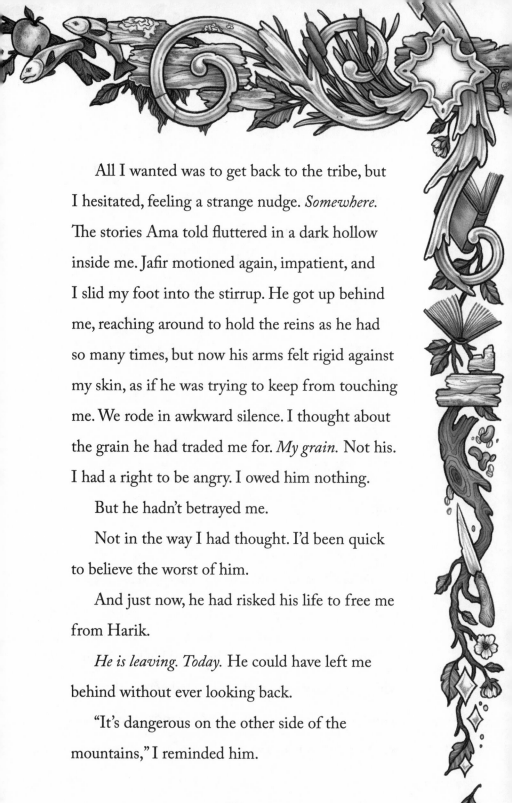

All I wanted was to get back to the tribe, but
I hesitated, feeling a strange nudge. *Somewhere.*
The stories Ama told fluttered in a dark hollow
inside me. Jafir motioned again, impatient, and
I slid my foot into the stirrup. He got up behind
me, reaching around to hold the reins as he had
so many times, but now his arms felt rigid against
my skin, as if he was trying to keep from touching
me. We rode in awkward silence. I thought about
the grain he had traded me for. *My grain.* Not his.
I had a right to be angry. I owed him nothing.

But he hadn't betrayed me.

Not in the way I had thought. I'd been quick
to believe the worst of him.

And just now, he had risked his life to free me
from Harik.

He is leaving. Today. He could have left me
behind without ever looking back.

"It's dangerous on the other side of the
mountains," I reminded him.

"It's dangerous here," he countered. I leaned back against his chest, forcing him to touch me. He cleared his throat. "Piers said he saw an ocean beyond the mountains when he was a boy."

"He must be the same age as Ama if he remembers it."

"He doesn't remember much. Only the blue. We'll look for that."

Blue. An ocean that might not even exist anymore. It was a fool's quest. And yet Ama's memories had fueled my own dreams for so very long.

Are there really such gardens, Ama?
Yes, my child, somewhere. And one day you will
find them.

Somewhere. One day. I brushed back the hair whipping across my face and gazed across the windblown, desolate landscape, a landscape that went on forever, and a new kind of despair seized

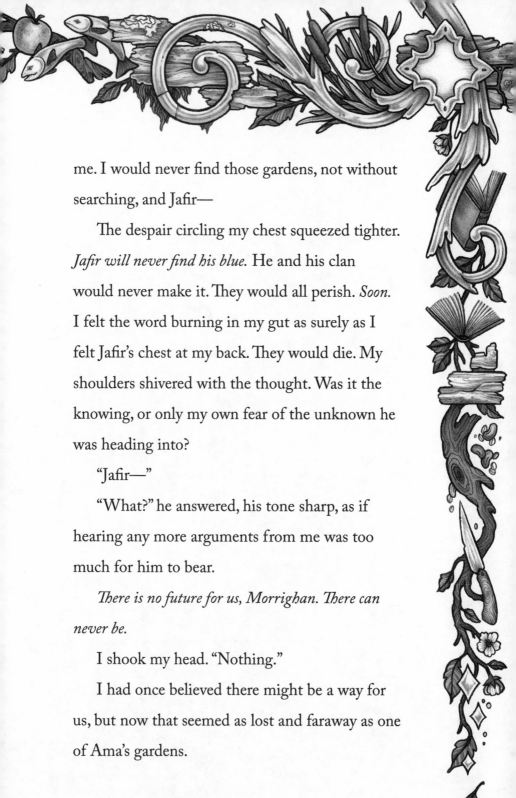

me. I would never find those gardens, not without searching, and Jafir—

The despair circling my chest squeezed tighter. *Jafir will never find his blue.* He and his clan would never make it. They would all perish. *Soon.* I felt the word burning in my gut as surely as I felt Jafir's chest at my back. They would die. My shoulders shivered with the thought. Was it the knowing, or only my own fear of the unknown he was heading into?

"Jafir—"

"What?" he answered, his tone sharp, as if hearing any more arguments from me was too much for him to bear.

There is no future for us, Morrighan. There can never be.

I shook my head. "Nothing."

I had once believed there might be a way for us, but now that seemed as lost and faraway as one of Ama's gardens.

CHAPTER TWENTY

MORRIGHAN

WE SAW IT AT THE SAME TIME. IT WAS A DUST
cloud rising behind a knoll, and in seconds, the
cloud became something else. A caravan. Horses
laden with packs. It looked like a small city,
though I already knew the numbers. Jafir had told
me. Twenty-five, eight of which were children.
They spotted us too, and seven of them broke
loose from the pack, a wild storm of hooves,
muscle, and madness heading toward us.

Jafir pulled back on the reins and muttered a
curse.

In seconds, they were upon us, their horses
frothing and stamping like man and beast were all

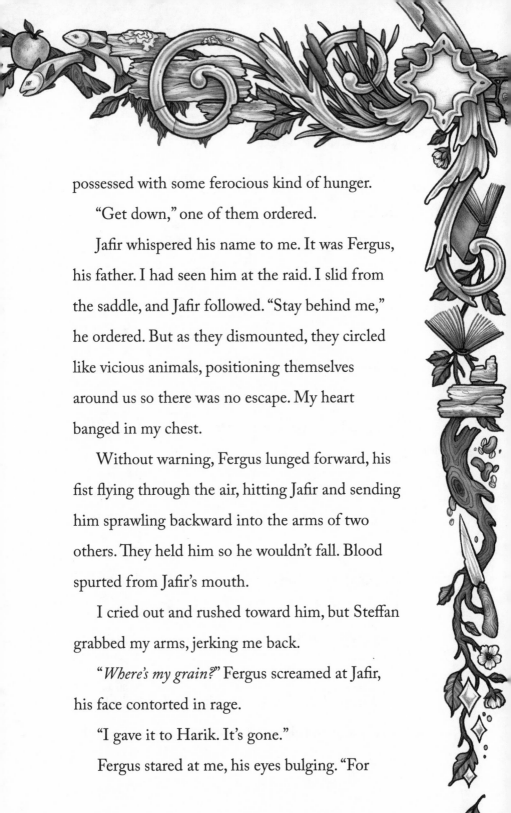

possessed with some ferocious kind of hunger.

"Get down," one of them ordered.

Jafir whispered his name to me. It was Fergus, his father. I had seen him at the raid. I slid from the saddle, and Jafir followed. "Stay behind me," he ordered. But as they dismounted, they circled like vicious animals, positioning themselves around us so there was no escape. My heart banged in my chest.

Without warning, Fergus lunged forward, his fist flying through the air, hitting Jafir and sending him sprawling backward into the arms of two others. They held him so he wouldn't fall. Blood spurted from Jafir's mouth.

I cried out and rushed toward him, but Steffan grabbed my arms, jerking me back.

"*Where's my grain?*" Fergus screamed at Jafir, his face contorted in rage.

"I gave it to Harik. It's gone."

Fergus stared at me, his eyes bulging. "For

her?" he yelled in disbelief. "You betrayed the clan for *her*?"

Jafir wiped his mouth with the back of his hand. "He and I made a deal. You are bound to honor it. Let her go, or you'll be defying him."

A snarl twisted across Fergus's face. "Honor disloyalty?" He laughed and walked over to me, shoving his face close to mine. His breath was sour, and his eyes were slivers of black glass. "You have the knowing, girl?"

I hesitated, not sure what I should say. I didn't owe this man the truth and was certain it wasn't wise to give him anything he wanted. Jafir watched me, misery in his eyes, and he shook his head slightly. *No.* I knew the message he was trying to send. If I had no worth, they might still let me go.

I looked at the crowd gathering behind him. The rest of the clan had caught up, a sea of gaunt stares. A baby cried. Another child whimpered.

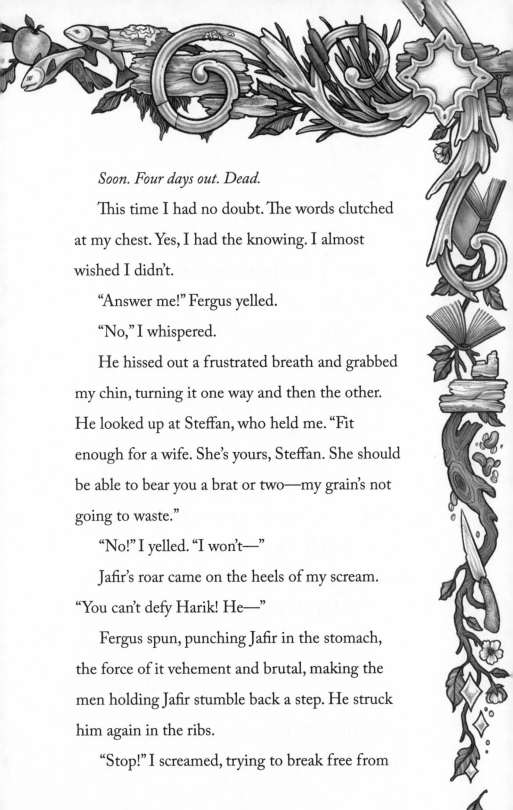

Soon. Four days out. Dead.

This time I had no doubt. The words clutched at my chest. Yes, I had the knowing. I almost wished I didn't.

"Answer me!" Fergus yelled.

"No," I whispered.

He hissed out a frustrated breath and grabbed my chin, turning it one way and then the other. He looked up at Steffan, who held me. "Fit enough for a wife. She's yours, Steffan. She should be able to bear you a brat or two—my grain's not going to waste."

"No!" I yelled. "I won't—"

Jafir's roar came on the heels of my scream. "You can't defy Harik! He—"

Fergus spun, punching Jafir in the stomach, the force of it vehement and brutal, making the men holding Jafir stumble back a step. He struck him again in the ribs.

"Stop!" I screamed, trying to break free from

Steffan, but his fingers were steel, digging into my arms. Jafir's head lolled to the side, his feet collapsing beneath him. Only the men holding his arms kept him from crumpling to the ground. Jafir coughed, spitting out blood.

"Like you defied me?" Fergus yelled. He grabbed Jafir's hair, pulling his head back so Jafir had to look at him. Jafir's blue eyes remained defiant.

"You betrayed the clan," Fergus growled. "You betrayed me. You stole food out of our mouths. You are no son of mine. Just like Liam was no brother." He drew his knife and held it to Jafir's neck.

"No!" I cried. "Please! Wait!"

Fergus looked back at me.

"Harik was right! I do have the knowing, and I am strong in it! That's why he wanted me," I said. "I'll guide you safely through the mountains and well past that, but only on one

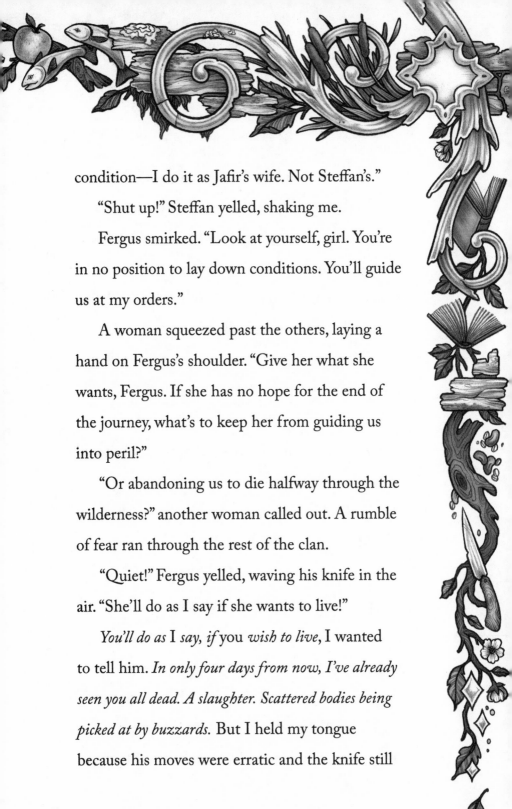

condition—I do it as Jafir's wife. Not Steffan's."

"Shut up!" Steffan yelled, shaking me.

Fergus smirked. "Look at yourself, girl. You're in no position to lay down conditions. You'll guide us at my orders."

A woman squeezed past the others, laying a hand on Fergus's shoulder. "Give her what she wants, Fergus. If she has no hope for the end of the journey, what's to keep her from guiding us into peril?"

"Or abandoning us to die halfway through the wilderness?" another woman called out. A rumble of fear ran through the rest of the clan.

"Quiet!" Fergus yelled, waving his knife in the air. "She'll do as I say if she wants to live!"

You'll do as I say, if you wish to live, I wanted to tell him. *In only four days from now, I've already seen you all dead. A slaughter. Scattered bodies being picked at by buzzards.* But I held my tongue because his moves were erratic and the knife still

waving in his hand far too close to Jafir's throat.

A large man stepped forward. He was taller and older than Fergus, a thick braid of white hair trailing down his back. "The way is uncertain. It would serve us all to have one of her kind helping to lead the way," he said. "But Laurida is right—if the girl has no hope for reward, it might spell our own doom."

Fergus took several pacing steps, as if weighing the man's words, and sheathed his knife. He surveyed the clan and their worried glances, then walked back to me, fingering the hair on my shoulder. "Very well, Morrighan of the Remnant. I'll strike a deal with you. If you lead us safely to a place of my liking and you please me with your helpfulness along the way, at the end of the journey, you will be Jafir's. If not, you will be Steffan's. Do you agree to this without argument?"

I knew there was no way I would ever please this man. He would never concede to my

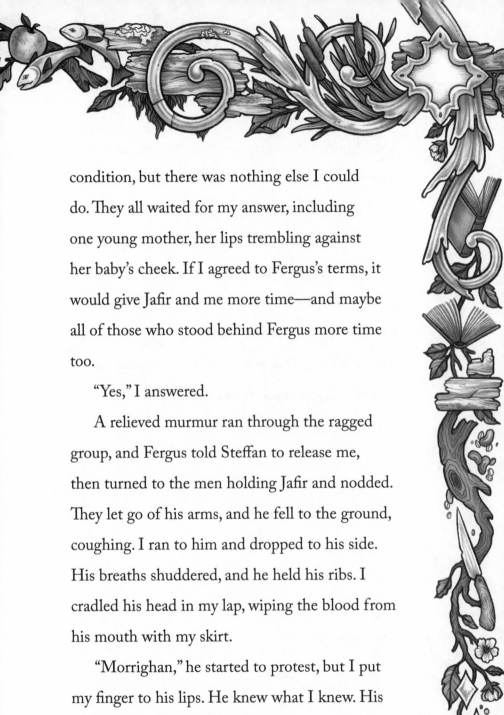

condition, but there was nothing else I could do. They all waited for my answer, including one young mother, her lips trembling against her baby's cheek. If I agreed to Fergus's terms, it would give Jafir and me more time—and maybe all of those who stood behind Fergus more time too.

"Yes," I answered.

A relieved murmur ran through the ragged group, and Fergus told Steffan to release me, then turned to the men holding Jafir and nodded. They let go of his arms, and he fell to the ground, coughing. I ran to him and dropped to his side. His breaths shuddered, and he held his ribs. I cradled his head in my lap, wiping the blood from his mouth with my skirt.

"Morrighan," he started to protest, but I put my finger to his lips. He knew what I knew. His father would give me nothing.

"Shh," I whispered. My vision blurred with

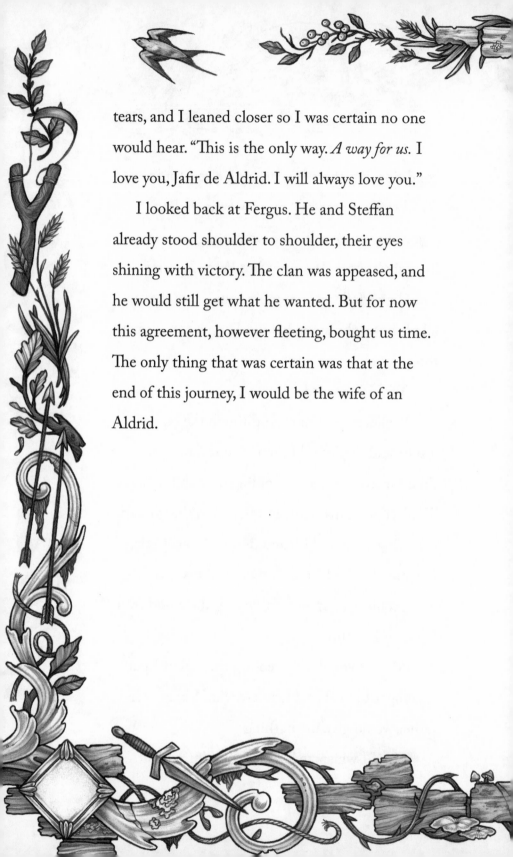

tears, and I leaned closer so I was certain no one would hear. "This is the only way. *A way for us.* I love you, Jafir de Aldrid. I will always love you."

I looked back at Fergus. He and Steffan already stood shoulder to shoulder, their eyes shining with victory. The clan was appeased, and he would still get what he wanted. But for now this agreement, however fleeting, bought us time. The only thing that was certain was that at the end of this journey, I would be the wife of an Aldrid.

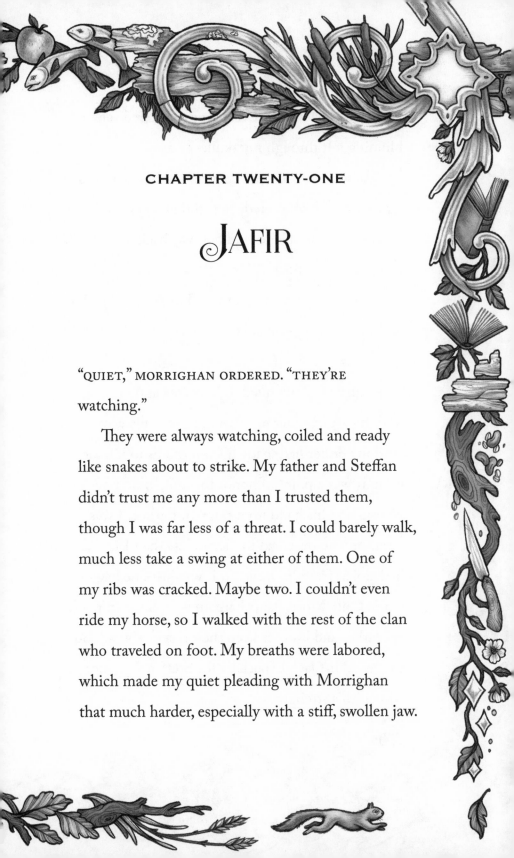

CHAPTER TWENTY-ONE

JAFIR

"QUIET," MORRIGHAN ORDERED. "THEY'RE watching."

They were always watching, coiled and ready like snakes about to strike. My father and Steffan didn't trust me any more than I trusted them, though I was far less of a threat. I could barely walk, much less take a swing at either of them. One of my ribs was cracked. Maybe two. I couldn't even ride my horse, so I walked with the rest of the clan who traveled on foot. My breaths were labored, which made my quiet pleading with Morrighan that much harder, especially with a stiff, swollen jaw.

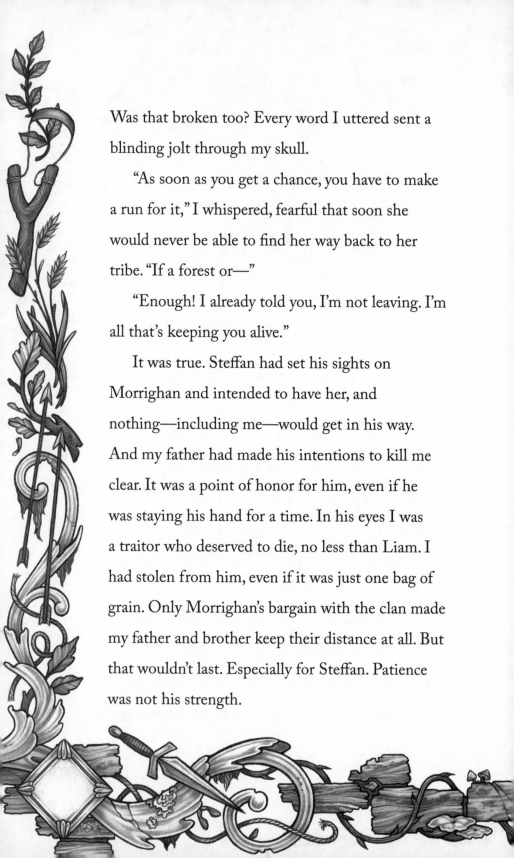

Was that broken too? Every word I uttered sent a blinding jolt through my skull.

"As soon as you get a chance, you have to make a run for it," I whispered, fearful that soon she would never be able to find her way back to her tribe. "If a forest or—"

"Enough! I already told you, I'm not leaving. I'm all that's keeping you alive."

It was true. Steffan had set his sights on Morrighan and intended to have her, and nothing—including me—would get in his way. And my father had made his intentions to kill me clear. It was a point of honor for him, even if he was staying his hand for a time. In his eyes I was a traitor who deserved to die, no less than Liam. I had stolen from him, even if it was just one bag of grain. Only Morrighan's bargain with the clan made my father and brother keep their distance at all. But that wouldn't last. Especially for Steffan. Patience was not his strength.

"Please—"

"Think of the children," she said to quiet me. She had whispered to me earlier that she sensed doom on the trail ahead. How could she know such things? It was not written in the sky or on the wind. Or was she only trying to sway me to silence?

Petra, Iris, and Skye, the three oldest children, walked ahead of us. The younger ones rode on top of supplies and bags of grain in the wagons. They all eyed Morrighan warily, along with their mothers. Most of them had heard of the knowing, the mysterious sense that some of those in the tribes possessed. Even the great Harik revered the knowing. Morrighan made it seem more natural and practical than magical. Back in our peaceful days in the meadow, she had tried to help me understand. *It's a way of perceiving as old as the universe. It is how the Ancients survived in those early years. When they lost everything else, they had to*

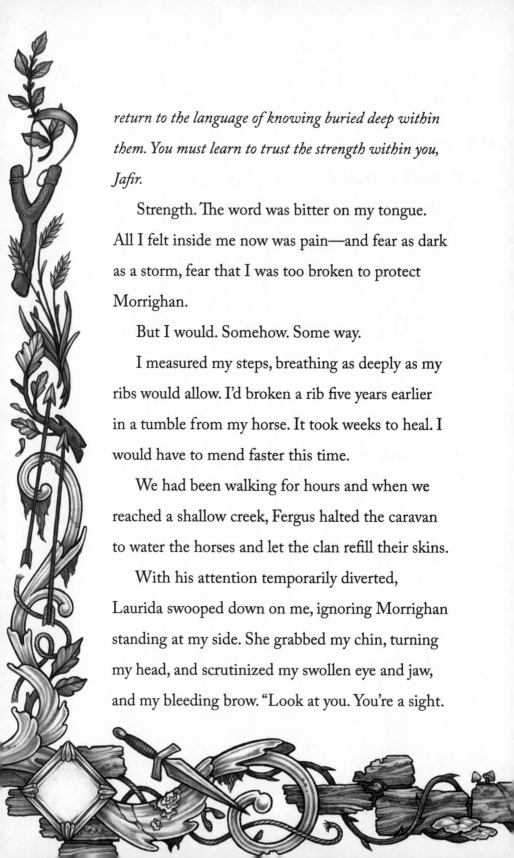

return to the language of knowing buried deep within them. You must learn to trust the strength within you, Jafir.

Strength. The word was bitter on my tongue. All I felt inside me now was pain—and fear as dark as a storm, fear that I was too broken to protect Morrighan.

But I would. Somehow. Some way.

I measured my steps, breathing as deeply as my ribs would allow. I'd broken a rib five years earlier in a tumble from my horse. It took weeks to heal. I would have to mend faster this time.

We had been walking for hours and when we reached a shallow creek, Fergus halted the caravan to water the horses and let the clan refill their skins.

With his attention temporarily diverted, Laurida swooped down on me, ignoring Morrighan standing at my side. She grabbed my chin, turning my head, and scrutinized my swollen eye and jaw, and my bleeding brow. "Look at you. You're a sight.

Not so pretty anymore, are you?" She briefly eyed Morrighan with distaste. "All of this for her? She has the bones of a bird. No strength in them. She's of no use at all! What were you thinking, Jafir?"

"She is strong in ways you can't see."

Laurida grunted, doubtful. "Don't defy him again, do you hear me? Or I will take a hand to you too." She glanced over her shoulder to make sure Fergus was still occupied at the creek. "Remember to breathe deeply, no matter how much it hurts, so your chest stays clear. And sleep propped up against a bag of grain. You will heal faster."

She turned to Morrighan at last. "Make yourself valuable, girl. Every minute of every day. Even if it takes lies and trickery. Your gods mean nothing to us, and they mean even less out there." She nodded toward the looming wilderness. "Your craftiness and cunning are all that will save you now."

CHAPTER TWENTY-TWO

ORRIGHAN

THREE DAYS WAS A LIFETIME. IT SEEMED WE HAD
been walking forever. There were no mercies in
Fergus, and he pushed animal and child alike at
a harsh pace, even in the summer heat. We had
passed over brown foothills separated by brown
valleys. They all looked the same. Shade was a rare
treasure. I had never traveled this far west before,
and now I knew why. It was as Ama said. A
terrible greatness had rolled across the land.

Sometimes I paused, listening, and Jafir would
ask, "What is it?" How could he and the others
not hear? The wilderness howled with desolation,
carrying the cries of the long dead, the millions

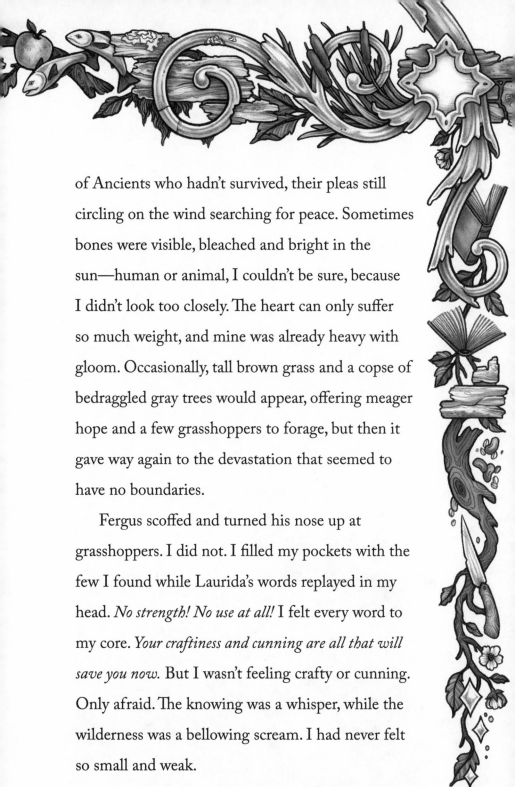

of Ancients who hadn't survived, their pleas still
circling on the wind searching for peace. Sometimes
bones were visible, bleached and bright in the
sun—human or animal, I couldn't be sure, because
I didn't look too closely. The heart can only suffer
so much weight, and mine was already heavy with
gloom. Occasionally, tall brown grass and a copse of
bedraggled gray trees would appear, offering meager
hope and a few grasshoppers to forage, but then it
gave way again to the devastation that seemed to
have no boundaries.

Fergus scoffed and turned his nose up at
grasshoppers. I did not. I filled my pockets with the
few I found while Laurida's words replayed in my
head. *No strength! No use at all!* I felt every word to
my core. *Your craftiness and cunning are all that will
save you now.* But I wasn't feeling crafty or cunning.
Only afraid. The knowing was a whisper, while the
wilderness was a bellowing scream. I had never felt
so small and weak.

I worried for Jafir and watched him incessantly, fearful his injuries would make him collapse. I saw the strain in his eyes, the effort it cost him to keep up. But each day I watched him gather a fierce strength within him too, one I hadn't seen before, refusing to rise to their baiting or give in to their callousness. How had he ever been able to overcome a lifetime of such cruelty? How had he ever found it within himself to show me mercy or kindness? It was for his sake that I reached deep

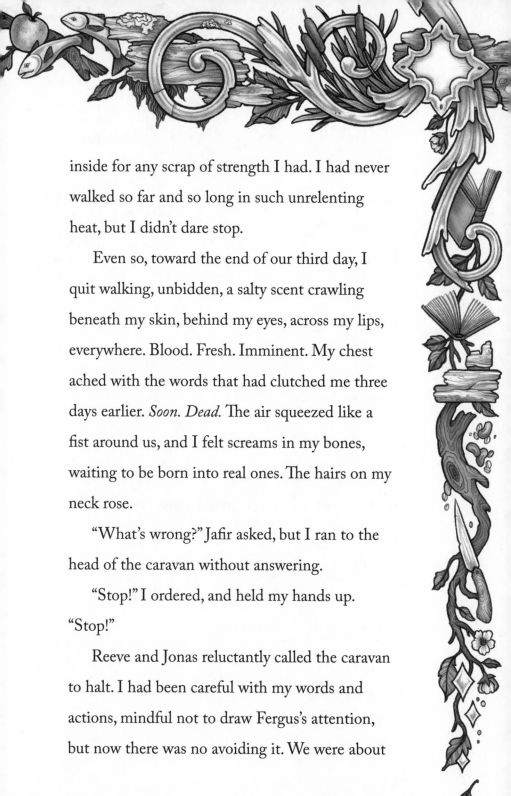

inside for any scrap of strength I had. I had never walked so far and so long in such unrelenting heat, but I didn't dare stop.

Even so, toward the end of our third day, I quit walking, unbidden, a salty scent crawling beneath my skin, behind my eyes, across my lips, everywhere. Blood. Fresh. Imminent. My chest ached with the words that had clutched me three days earlier. *Soon. Dead.* The air squeezed like a fist around us, and I felt screams in my bones, waiting to be born into real ones. The hairs on my neck rose.

"What's wrong?" Jafir asked, but I ran to the head of the caravan without answering.

"Stop!" I ordered, and held my hands up. "Stop!"

Reeve and Jonas reluctantly called the caravan to halt. I had been careful with my words and actions, mindful not to draw Fergus's attention, but now there was no avoiding it. We were about

to descend into a valley. Fergus was instantly at the head of the caravan too, his horse prancing, impatient. "Not this way," I said. "North. We have to turn north. *Now.*"

His eyes lit with reprisal. It was as if he had been waiting for this moment. He got down from his horse and though he stood almost toe to toe with me, he spoke loudly so everyone would hear. "For what purpose, girl? This is the fastest way," he said, pointing down to the valley. "I see thick groves of trees ahead that will offer us shade. The north is cold and treacherous. I think you're trying to mislead us for your own—"

"I'm warning you," I said firmly, "there is danger ahead. There are many kinds of scavengers in these lands. And that route—"

"Fergus," Reeve whispered. "I see something."

Piers rode forward, squinting into the distance. "Smoke," he confirmed. The clan edged closer. A thin line of smoke wriggled up from the horizon.

Only two things created fires—lightning and people. There were no clouds in the sky.

"What kind of people would be way out here in this wilderness?" Glynis asked, pulling close to Piers.

"Predators," Tory called out.

Glynis and Piers both nodded agreement.

"It could be travelers, just like us," Fergus snapped.

"But *she knew*," Laurida said. "She was at the back of the caravan, and before anyone else saw the smoke, she knew, and sensed danger."

Fergus glared at her, but a restless mumble was already running through the clan.

He turned back to me, his face dark, and he grabbed my arm, wrenching me away with a jerk.

"No!" It was Jafir, but Christo and Jonas seized him from behind and held him back while Fergus dragged me to a high stand of brush where no one could see us.

He kept his voice low, but it was as sharp and dangerous as a blade. "There is only one person in this clan who chooses our routes. *One.* If you get some crazy omen in that head of yours, you will come to me in private. You will not blather out orders in front of the whole clan! I alone decide. *Me.*"

"There wasn't time to come to you in private. I don't know these lands either. I have no map. Only a sense inside that I have to trust!"

"Then this sense better come to you with more notice. Do you understand?"

I nodded.

His fingers dug into my arm, and when I winced, he threw me to the ground. My arms splayed wide on the loose rock, and my cheek hit hard on the scrabble.

"Get up!" he ordered.

I got to my feet, holding my face, feeling the wet warmth of blood.

"Shame you lost your footing, isn't it? You're a clumsy thing. That is what you will tell Jafir."

I nodded, his message clear. He was in charge, even ruling over my words, and no blame should ever be pointed toward him, or I would pay a greater price. Or, worse, Jafir would.

He stormed off, but I heard him tell the clan *his* decision. We would turn north.

Days turned to weeks, weeks to months. The supplies ran out long before our journey did. Food became as scarce as courage. Game was rare, and when it was to be found, it was almost always Jafir who snared it or brought it down with an arrow. He had healed from his injuries and was still the best hunter of the clan, but even rabbits and birds were hard to come by in a barren landscape.

Everyone turned to me for guidance, expecting me to know everything. *Where is it? Where is the game? The seed? The nuts?* I didn't know. Laurida's warning pounded inside me: *Make yourself valuable, even if it takes lies. It is all that will save you.*

I helped her prepare and cook what little food there was, but as I did, I eyed her knives, which I was not allowed to use, being relegated only to plucking feathers or fetching water. She kept the two knives wrapped in rough cloth. One was dull and chipped. *Useless,* Laurida called it, her same opinion of me on our first meeting.

"Then why do you keep it?" I asked.

"Because it is better than having nothing at all."

Nothing. That is what I felt like, a useless chipped knife kept as a last resort. A last resort for what? More of nothing is what the following weeks rolled into, but I forced myself to find other ways to make myself valuable.

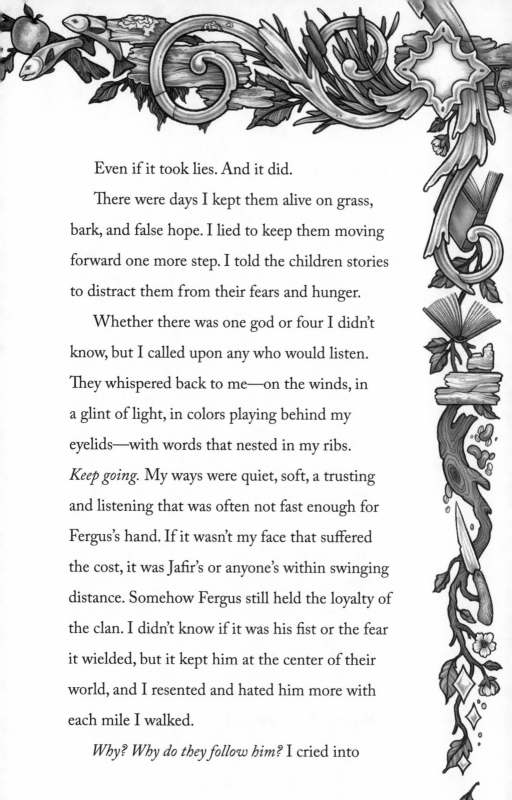

Even if it took lies. And it did.

There were days I kept them alive on grass, bark, and false hope. I lied to keep them moving forward one more step. I told the children stories to distract them from their fears and hunger.

Whether there was one god or four I didn't know, but I called upon any who would listen. They whispered back to me—on the winds, in a glint of light, in colors playing behind my eyelids—with words that nested in my ribs. *Keep going.* My ways were quiet, soft, a trusting and listening that was often not fast enough for Fergus's hand. If it wasn't my face that suffered the cost, it was Jafir's or anyone's within swinging distance. Somehow Fergus still held the loyalty of the clan. I didn't know if it was his fist or the fear it wielded, but it kept him at the center of their world, and I resented and hated him more with each mile I walked.

Why? Why do they follow him? I cried into

Jafir's chest more than once when we dared to steal a secret moment.

His answer was always the same. *He has kept them alive all these years. That is all they know. All that matters. They are alive because of him. They won't forget that.*

They are alive in spite of him, I thought.

I mourned for the gentleness of my tribe, and at times thought I couldn't go on, but Ama was right. It was in the sorrows, in the fear, in the need, that the knowing gained flight, and I had much of all these. I remembered that eight-year-old girl I had once been, the one who had cowered between boulders, waiting to die. In my years spent with the tribe, I thought I understood fear. I thought I knew loss.

I didn't.

Not in the way I knew now.

We lost baby Jules to a beast. It came out of nowhere, swift and vicious. We didn't know what

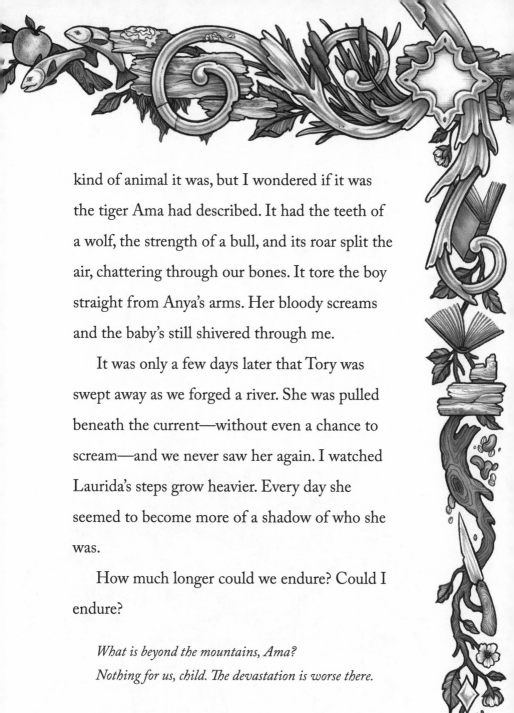

kind of animal it was, but I wondered if it was the tiger Ama had described. It had the teeth of a wolf, the strength of a bull, and its roar split the air, chattering through our bones. It tore the boy straight from Anya's arms. Her bloody screams and the baby's still shivered through me.

It was only a few days later that Tory was swept away as we forged a river. She was pulled beneath the current—without even a chance to scream—and we never saw her again. I watched Laurida's steps grow heavier. Every day she seemed to become more of a shadow of who she was.

How much longer could we endure? Could I endure?

What is beyond the mountains, Ama?
Nothing for us, child. The devastation is worse there.

With every passing day, my hope for a world with green gardens and trees heavy with red fruit

dimmed. I watched the children grow weaker.
Pale. And then the snow flurries began. Winter
was upon us.

I became someone I barely knew anymore.

My desperation grew teeth. Claws. It became
an animal inside me that knew no bounds,
unspeakable, just as Jafir had tried to explain to
me so long ago. It tore open my darkest thoughts,

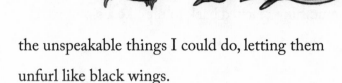

the unspeakable things I could do, letting them
unfurl like black wings.

I watched Jafir change too. His soft face grew
hard, his eyes sharp. Enduring his clan's rough
ways was something he had grown used to, but
watching me endure them seemed to be more
than he could bear. Every day I feared he would
snap and Fergus would kill him once and for all.
I couldn't convince him to be afraid for himself,
but I knew he was always afraid for me. In those
moments, when I thought he was about to spring,
I would remind him, *If you are dead, I become
Steffan's.*

One dark day, when metal-gray skies blocked
the sun and the miles before us were still endless,
my knees gave way and I fell to the ground on
all fours, too tired, too worn, too broken to even
sob. Empty. I sensed a muffled clamor around
me, voices trying to coax me up, but I remained
on all fours staring at the ground, numb, reaching

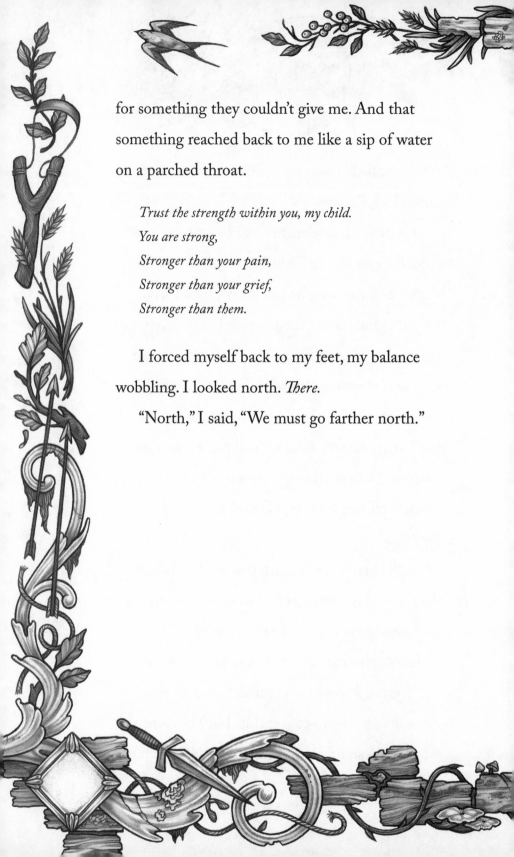

for something they couldn't give me. And that
something reached back to me like a sip of water
on a parched throat.

> *Trust the strength within you, my child.*
> *You are strong,*
> *Stronger than your pain,*
> *Stronger than your grief,*
> *Stronger than them.*

I forced myself back to my feet, my balance
wobbling. I looked north. *There.*

"North," I said, "We must go farther north."

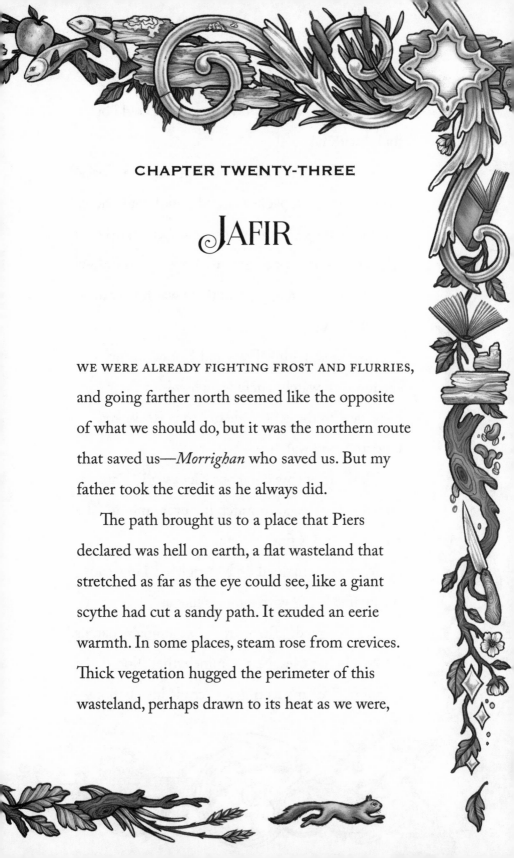

CHAPTER TWENTY-THREE

JAFIR

WE WERE ALREADY FIGHTING FROST AND FLURRIES, and going farther north seemed like the opposite of what we should do, but it was the northern route that saved us—*Morrighan* who saved us. But my father took the credit as he always did.

The path brought us to a place that Piers declared was hell on earth, a flat wasteland that stretched as far as the eye could see, like a giant scythe had cut a sandy path. It exuded an eerie warmth. In some places, steam rose from crevices. Thick vegetation hugged the perimeter of this wasteland, perhaps drawn to its heat as we were,

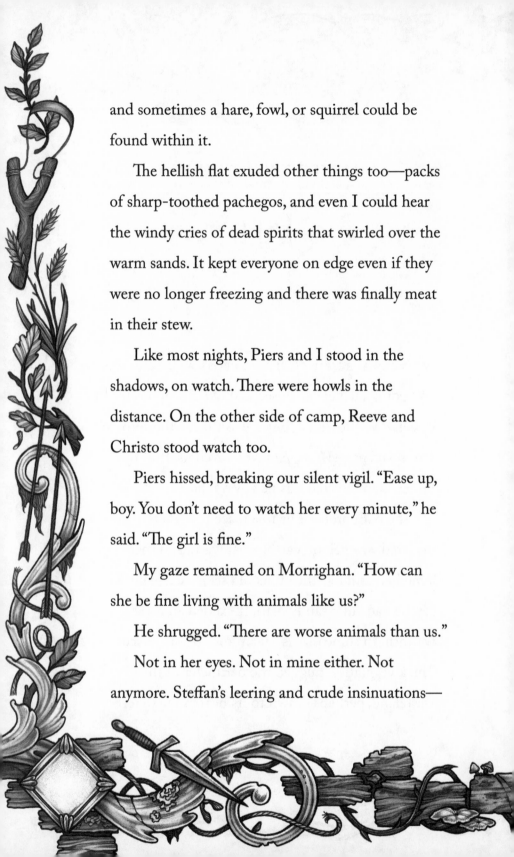

and sometimes a hare, fowl, or squirrel could be found within it.

The hellish flat exuded other things too—packs of sharp-toothed pachegos, and even I could hear the windy cries of dead spirits that swirled over the warm sands. It kept everyone on edge even if they were no longer freezing and there was finally meat in their stew.

Like most nights, Piers and I stood in the shadows, on watch. There were howls in the distance. On the other side of camp, Reeve and Christo stood watch too.

Piers hissed, breaking our silent vigil. "Ease up, boy. You don't need to watch her every minute," he said. "The girl is fine."

My gaze remained on Morrighan. "How can she be fine living with animals like us?"

He shrugged. "There are worse animals than us."

Not in her eyes. Not in mine either. Not anymore. Steffan's leering and crude insinuations—

some days it took all my strength not to cut out his tongue and eyes. He watched her as if counting the days until she was his. When he made a quick move to touch her hair or waist like she was a mare he was trying to tame, she elbowed or kicked him, and he laughed like it was a game. *One day she will beg for my touch*, he'd say to taunt me. *I will make her beg.*

I'd kill him first. More than once, Morrighan had held me back. *Patience*, she would whisper. *He wants you to force Fergus's hand. And Fergus still holds the loyalty of the clan.*

The metal stewpot and bowls that Laurida and Morrighan were packing back in the wagon clanged and rattled. "Quiet over there!" Fergus snarled from his bedroll.

Laurida loudly banged one more pot before the camp was silent again. I had snagged game today, not much to feed so many—three bony squirrels and a long fat snake—but it was something, and every bit of food mattered.

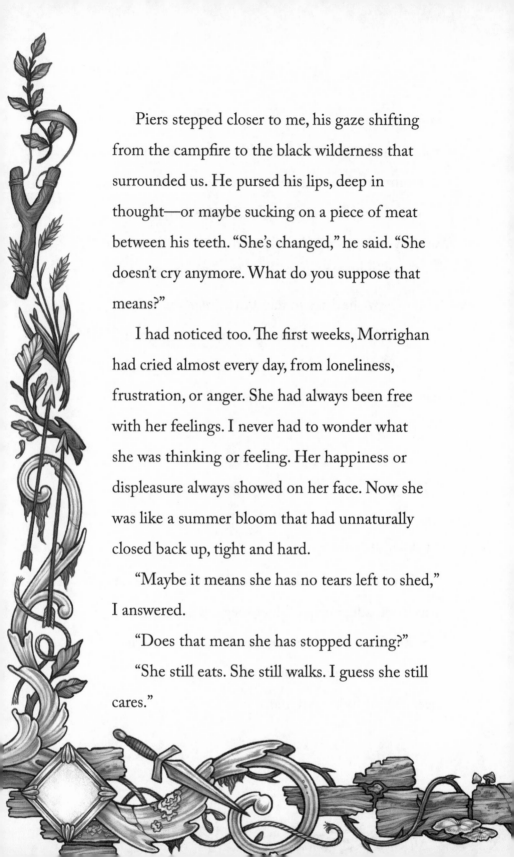

Piers stepped closer to me, his gaze shifting from the campfire to the black wilderness that surrounded us. He pursed his lips, deep in thought—or maybe sucking on a piece of meat between his teeth. "She's changed," he said. "She doesn't cry anymore. What do you suppose that means?"

I had noticed too. The first weeks, Morrighan had cried almost every day, from loneliness, frustration, or anger. She had always been free with her feelings. I never had to wonder what she was thinking or feeling. Her happiness or displeasure always showed on her face. Now she was like a summer bloom that had unnaturally closed back up, tight and hard.

"Maybe it means she has no tears left to shed," I answered.

"Does that mean she has stopped caring?"

"She still eats. She still walks. I guess she still cares."

But it seemed her hold on this world was growing thin.

"Morrighan," Elzy called softly, jiggling a fussing child on her hip. The children whimpered, the darkness too heavy, the howls too close. It had become almost routine. *Please, come tell the children a story. A story of Before.* Morrighan always complied, but I was the only one who heard the ache in her voice. The longing. I knew with every word she was reminded of her tribe and those she would never see again. My own throat throbbed with what we had done to her. If I could turn back the days, I never would have returned to the meadow, never would have kissed her, never—

I shook my head, knowing I was lying to myself, because with my last breath, I knew I would always be trying to find a way for us. But the timing was as agonizing as having the skin peeled from my bones. I was learning patience from her, just as I had learned so many other things, like learning how to love.

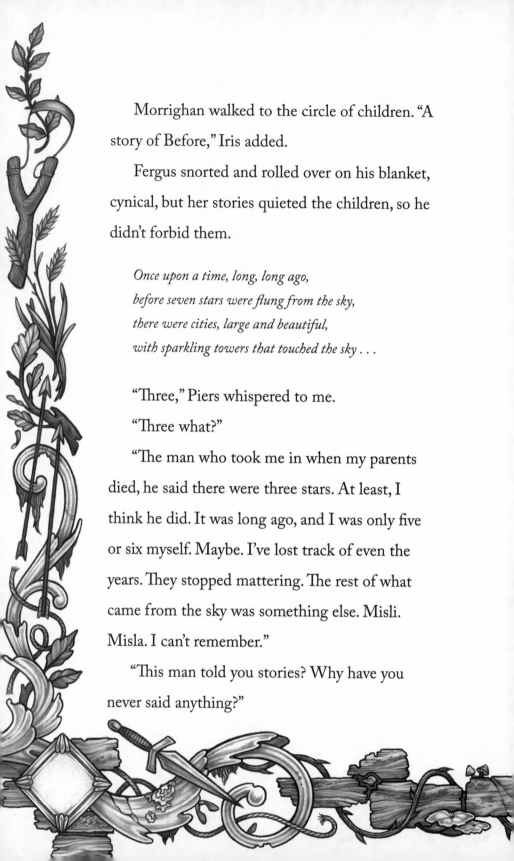

Morrighan walked to the circle of children. "A story of Before," Iris added.

Fergus snorted and rolled over on his blanket, cynical, but her stories quieted the children, so he didn't forbid them.

Once upon a time, long, long ago,
before seven stars were flung from the sky,
there were cities, large and beautiful,
with sparkling towers that touched the sky . . .

"Three," Piers whispered to me.

"Three what?"

"The man who took me in when my parents died, he said there were three stars. At least, I think he did. It was long ago, and I was only five or six myself. Maybe. I've lost track of even the years. They stopped mattering. The rest of what came from the sky was something else. Misli. Misla. I can't remember."

"This man told you stories? Why have you never said anything?"

"They weren't stories. I only remember a frightened man, desperate to tell me everything about the world, what had happened, the way it had been. None of it made much sense. When he wasn't telling me, he was writing it down, but there weren't enough days. He died of some sickness, and I was left alone to wander. Mostly starving. That's when I banded together with Fergus's father and other boys like us left on their own. Together we were strong. We roamed the ruins, finding or taking what we could. Otherwise, we would have died."

"What did the world look like Before? Were there really sparkling towers?"

He nodded as he stared at the campfire. "I lived in one. I remember that much. And I remember cupboards full of dishes. So many shiny dishes. I wonder sometimes if my parents were rich. And from my window I could see a line of blue. An ocean. The memories are blurred—hazy,

like a dream—but I remember going down to a shore and breathing in cool briny air, feeling waves lap at my ankles, the bubbles, the sticky saltiness on my cheeks. Or maybe those are only dreams. Things the old man told me. Who knows?"

"What about your parents? Do you remember them?"

He shook his head, a slight wince around his eyes that the darkness couldn't mask. "Maybe I was younger than I thought. Or maybe everything that came after wiped those memories away." He turned and looked at me, the campfire lighting the side of his face, his expression hollow. "I've done things I wish I hadn't, but then sometimes we do what we must, in order to survive. You should tell her that. Survival sometimes comes at great cost."

"Cost to who?"

"Everyone. Everyone pays. But only the

ruthless and shrewd survive."

I didn't reply. I was sick of the costs already. Both of us returned to our watch, our silent thoughts, and the occasional cry of a pachego in the distance, but his words wore on me. I paced the perimeters of our camp, trying to dispel them, but they followed after me, nipping at my back like sharp-toothed creatures. *Only the ruthless and shrewd survive. Tell her that.* Did he think Morrighan was going to die? Or was he trying to tell her to survive at all costs?

I stopped pacing and listened to her as she finished her story, her cheeks flushed with the heat of the campfire. She rose from her spot on the dirt and said good night to the sleepy children while Elzy and the other mothers huddled them together under the wagon. When she turned, her eyes met mine, golden in the firelight.

"Go," Piers said, motioning toward

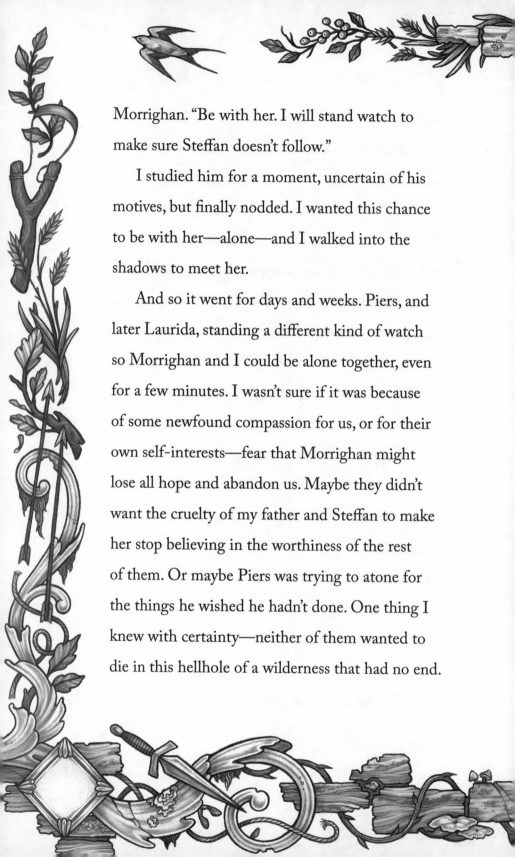

Morrighan. "Be with her. I will stand watch to make sure Steffan doesn't follow."

I studied him for a moment, uncertain of his motives, but finally nodded. I wanted this chance to be with her—alone—and I walked into the shadows to meet her.

And so it went for days and weeks. Piers, and later Laurida, standing a different kind of watch so Morrighan and I could be alone together, even for a few minutes. I wasn't sure if it was because of some newfound compassion for us, or for their own self-interests—fear that Morrighan might lose all hope and abandon us. Maybe they didn't want the cruelty of my father and Steffan to make her stop believing in the worthiness of the rest of them. Or maybe Piers was trying to atone for the things he wished he hadn't done. One thing I knew with certainty—neither of them wanted to die in this hellhole of a wilderness that had no end.

CHAPTER TWENTY-FOUR

MORRIGHAN

JAFIR'S LIPS TRAILED DOWN MY NECK LIKE A SILKY waterfall. His hands slipped beneath my shirt, calloused, rough, cut and scraped from a wilderness that was breaking us day by day, a journey that was crushing us, but his touch was gentle, reverent in the way that was only Jafir. He traced the lines of my back, circling around to caress my breasts, trembling, exploring, needing.

Tenderness. It was food in our stomachs. Medicine to our souls.

I closed my eyes, pretending it was before, my fingers skimming upward over the muscles of

his abdomen and then his chest. Our days in the meadow seemed a lifetime ago instead of months. Those days were a distant dream now, a time when we were still as fresh and green as spring grass. That was not who we were anymore. Still, our breaths mingled and I was astonished anew at this thing that was us.

A tear rolled down my cheek with the remembering, and I was grateful for the darkness and what he couldn't see. My throat swelled. "Kiss me, Jafir," I whispered. "Kiss me the way—"

His mouth was on mine. Hard. Hungry.

Desperate. Like he was trying to erase where we were and what we had become, something as wild and feral as the pachegos. I couldn't see his eyes, the crystal blue that fed my soul, but I was certain there were tears in them too.

We dropped to the ground on the blanket he had spread, and his mouth, his touch, grew more urgent, like the life we had in the canyon couldn't

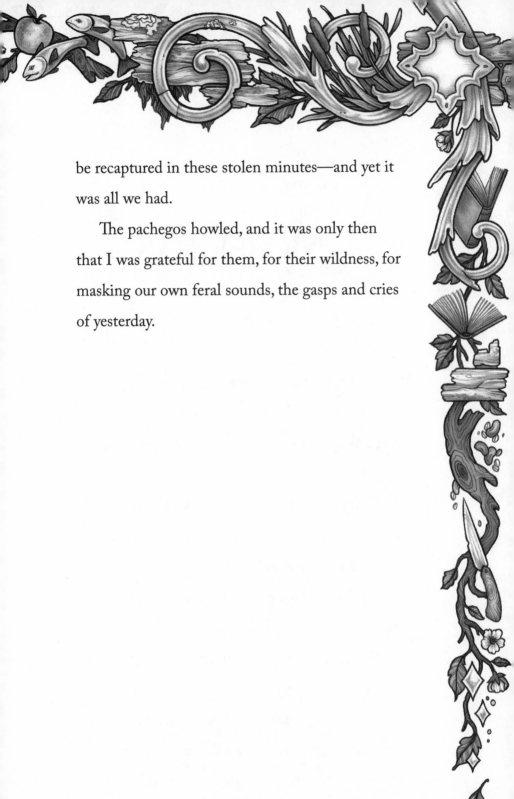

be recaptured in these stolen minutes—and yet it was all we had.

The pachegos howled, and it was only then that I was grateful for them, for their wildness, for masking our own feral sounds, the gasps and cries of yesterday.

CHAPTER TWENTY-FIVE

MORRIGHAN

"GET DOWN ON YOUR KNEES," FERGUS ORDERED. "Beg. Do whatever you have to do. Just get the guard to open the gate, then slash his throat. We'll do the rest."

Laurida didn't argue, but I saw the terror in her eyes. She took the small, sharp knife Fergus gave her and hid it in her skirts.

Fergus had become obsessed ever since he spotted the fortress on the hill.

We left the sandy wastelands weeks ago and began encountering steep hills that grew thicker with forests. And then we descended into a valley that had an enormous circle of trees with trunks

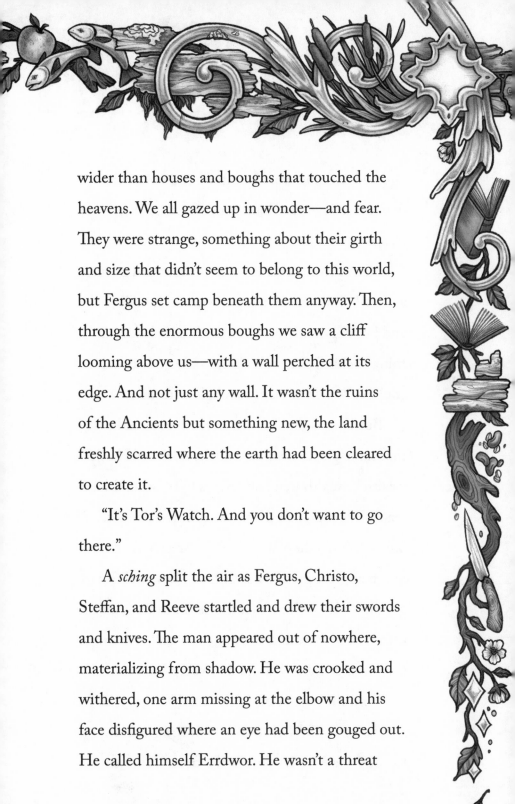

wider than houses and boughs that touched the heavens. We all gazed up in wonder—and fear. They were strange, something about their girth and size that didn't seem to belong to this world, but Fergus set camp beneath them anyway. Then, through the enormous boughs we saw a cliff looming above us—with a wall perched at its edge. And not just any wall. It wasn't the ruins of the Ancients but something new, the land freshly scarred where the earth had been cleared to create it.

"It's Tor's Watch. And you don't want to go there."

A *sching* split the air as Fergus, Christo, Steffan, and Reeve startled and drew their swords and knives. The man appeared out of nowhere, materializing from shadow. He was crooked and withered, one arm missing at the elbow and his face disfigured where an eye had been gouged out. He called himself Errdwor. He wasn't a threat

and had nothing worth stealing, and once they determined he was alone, they sheathed their weapons.

He explained that it was a fortress and a cruel and evil family lived behind its wall. "A widow and her children. Sorcerers, the bunch. They have things behind that wall, things only gods could conjure. You don't want to tangle with them."

But Fergus did. I saw it in his eyes already, that same gleam he had when he spoke of Harik's wealth—wealth that had always been beyond his reach. But this time there wasn't a river to cross, only a hill to climb and a wall to breach. And his numbers were greater now. I hated how well I was getting to know him, that his dark machinations unfolded in my mind so easily, especially when there was nothing I could do to stop him.

"And the master of the fortress?"

"Long dead." Errdwor spit on the ground to emphasize his hatred for the man. "He was

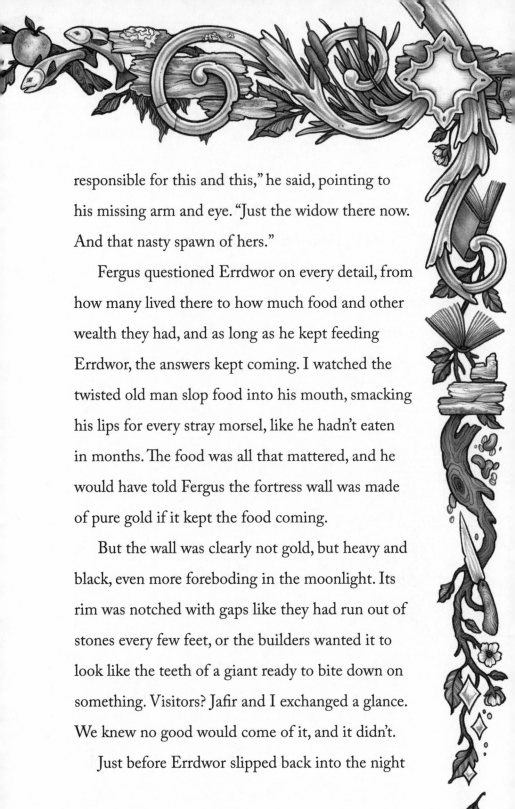

responsible for this and this," he said, pointing to his missing arm and eye. "Just the widow there now. And that nasty spawn of hers."

Fergus questioned Errdwor on every detail, from how many lived there to how much food and other wealth they had, and as long as he kept feeding Errdwor, the answers kept coming. I watched the twisted old man slop food into his mouth, smacking his lips for every stray morsel, like he hadn't eaten in months. The food was all that mattered, and he would have told Fergus the fortress wall was made of pure gold if it kept the food coming.

But the wall was clearly not gold, but heavy and black, even more foreboding in the moonlight. Its rim was notched with gaps like they had run out of stones every few feet, or the builders wanted it to look like the teeth of a giant ready to bite down on something. Visitors? Jafir and I exchanged a glance. We knew no good would come of it, and it didn't.

Just before Errdwor slipped back into the night

as quickly as he had come, he claimed there was only one guard and a dozen or so others who were holed up behind the wall. By morning, Fergus had already laid out his plans for a raid. He said with fourteen of us armed and surprise on our side, they didn't have a chance. Anya and Elzy and two of the other young mothers were left down below with the children, but every other member of the clan hid in the surrounding forest—including me. Fergus didn't trust me enough to leave me behind.

As I watched them move into place like calculating wolves, I remembered their raid in the vale . . . the screams, the panic, the cold, systematic gutting of our home—the ruthlessness. Now I would be part of this raid.

My stomach rolled, and bile crawled up my throat. Jafir's sorrowful words surfaced. *I had no choice, I had to ride with them. I tried to steer them off course.*

Steer them off course? Was that even possible?

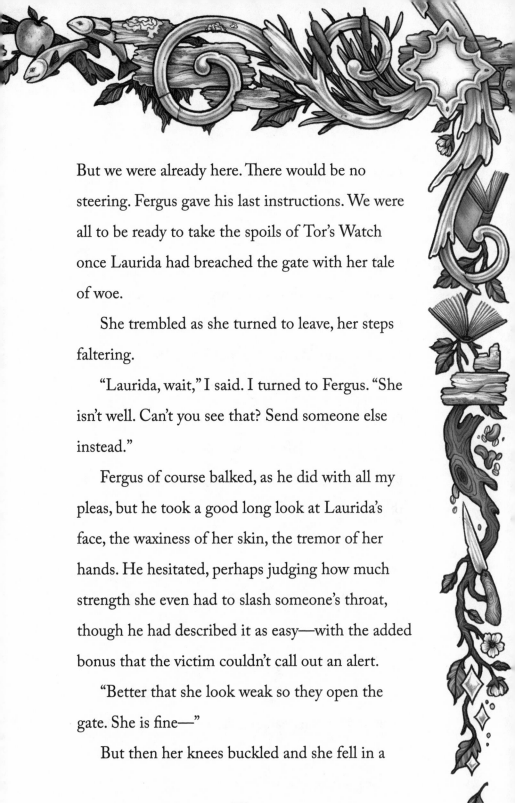

But we were already here. There would be no steering. Fergus gave his last instructions. We were all to be ready to take the spoils of Tor's Watch once Laurida had breached the gate with her tale of woe.

She trembled as she turned to leave, her steps faltering.

"Laurida, wait," I said. I turned to Fergus. "She isn't well. Can't you see that? Send someone else instead."

Fergus of course balked, as he did with all my pleas, but he took a good long look at Laurida's face, the waxiness of her skin, the tremor of her hands. He hesitated, perhaps judging how much strength she even had to slash someone's throat, though he had described it as easy—with the added bonus that the victim couldn't call out an alert.

"Better that she look weak so they open the gate. She is fine—"

But then her knees buckled and she fell in a

heap to the ground. I dropped to her side and
held a waterskin to her lips. She moaned and
Fergus cursed.

Jafir left his position, rushing to her side.
"Take her back down to camp," Fergus ordered.
Jafir scooped her into his arms, his attention torn
between Laurida and me, but I nodded, urging
him to go. Before Jafir carried her away, Fergus
pulled his small knife from her skirt pocket and,
when he heard Jafir's horse leave, shoved it into
my hand. He didn't need to say why—I was to be
the "someone else."

"No muscle on you. A weak, useless thing you
are." Disgust twisted his face. "They won't hesitate
to open the gate for you. Do *exactly* what I told
her to do. I'll be watching."

"I'll be watching too." Steffan had moved
from his position in the forest to his father's side.
"Remember the deal. You are to please us both."

Steffan's eyes said more than his words,

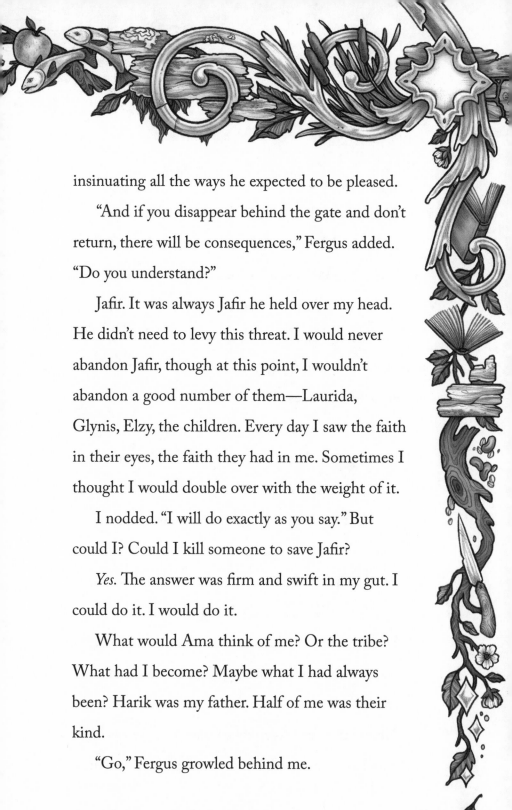

insinuating all the ways he expected to be pleased.

"And if you disappear behind the gate and don't return, there will be consequences," Fergus added. "Do you understand?"

Jafir. It was always Jafir he held over my head. He didn't need to levy this threat. I would never abandon Jafir, though at this point, I wouldn't abandon a good number of them—Laurida, Glynis, Elzy, the children. Every day I saw the faith in their eyes, the faith they had in me. Sometimes I thought I would double over with the weight of it.

I nodded. "I will do exactly as you say." But could I? Could I kill someone to save Jafir?

Yes. The answer was firm and swift in my gut. I could do it. I would do it.

What would Ama think of me? Or the tribe? What had I become? Maybe what I had always been? Harik was my father. Half of me was their kind.

"Go," Fergus growled behind me.

I walked out of the cover of the forest and up the steep, barren trail that led to the fortress entrance. My heart hammered in my chest. The black stone wall was the height of two tall men. How had a dozen people ever managed to build such a large barrier from heavy stone? It looked like something imagined from one of Ama's embellished tales.

I picked up a large rock and used it to bang on the iron gate. It echoed heavy and ominous.

"What do you want?"

I put my ear to the gate, unsure where the voice came from.

"Up here," the voice called.

I stepped back, and when I looked up, my breath went still. Standing in one of the notches was an old woman wearing a brown cloak. How she had appeared there so quickly, I didn't know. Her white hair was streaked with tinges of yellow and flowed in a neat braid over her shoulder. The

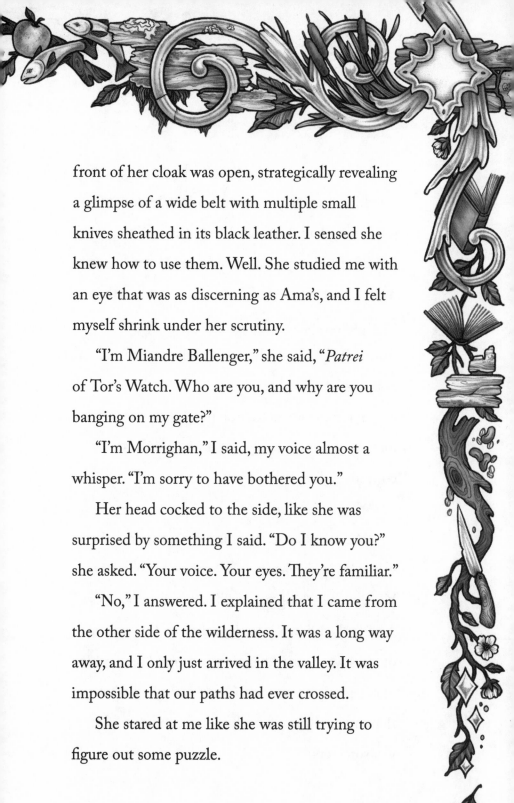

front of her cloak was open, strategically revealing a glimpse of a wide belt with multiple small knives sheathed in its black leather. I sensed she knew how to use them. Well. She studied me with an eye that was as discerning as Ama's, and I felt myself shrink under her scrutiny.

"I'm Miandre Ballenger," she said, "*Patrei* of Tor's Watch. Who are you, and why are you banging on my gate?"

"I'm Morrighan," I said, my voice almost a whisper. "I'm sorry to have bothered you."

Her head cocked to the side, like she was surprised by something I said. "Do I know you?" she asked. "Your voice. Your eyes. They're familiar."

"No," I answered. I explained that I came from the other side of the wilderness. It was a long way away, and I only just arrived in the valley. It was impossible that our paths had ever crossed.

She stared at me like she was still trying to figure out some puzzle.

Minutes were passing, and I knew Fergus was watching, probably shifting his feet, impatient, wondering why I wasn't already through the gate. I cried out loudly so he could hear. "I need your help! Please let me in." But in my next breath, I mouthed, *No. No.* My warning to her came instinctively. Maybe I couldn't kill someone as easily as I'd thought.

Her eyes narrowed. She perceived my silent message and said softly, "And what of those cowards hiding behind you?"

"You saw them?"

"We saw you all the minute you entered this valley. We saw when you set camp down below. We see everything you do. There is little we miss."

I looked down into the valley and the crown of trees we camped beneath and could see nothing of our group or wagons. Could her eyes be better than mine? I turned back to her, confused. "Are you sorcerers?"

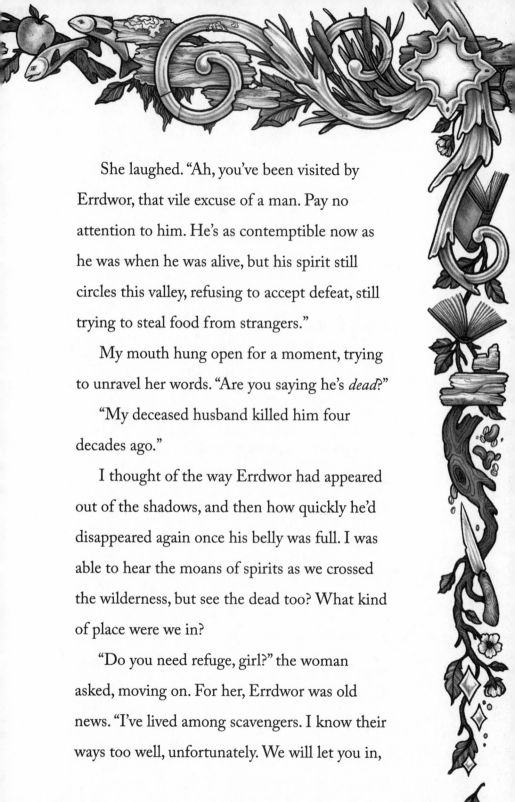

She laughed. "Ah, you've been visited by Errdwor, that vile excuse of a man. Pay no attention to him. He's as contemptible now as he was when he was alive, but his spirit still circles this valley, refusing to accept defeat, still trying to steal food from strangers."

My mouth hung open for a moment, trying to unravel her words. "Are you saying he's *dead*?"

"My deceased husband killed him four decades ago."

I thought of the way Errdwor had appeared out of the shadows, and then how quickly he'd disappeared again once his belly was full. I was able to hear the moans of spirits as we crossed the wilderness, but see the dead too? What kind of place were we in?

"Do you need refuge, girl?" the woman asked, moving on. For her, Errdwor was old news. "I've lived among scavengers. I know their ways too well, unfortunately. We will let you in,

but you'll have to leave that knife behind."

I stared at her, at first bewildered, but then my chest rose in a long, guilty breath. How much could this woman see?

She smiled. "Your skirt—the one side hangs heavy. Something's weighing it down. I told you. I know the scavengers' ways."

"I can't come in," I said, shaking my head. I told her about the others I couldn't leave behind and my promise to lead them to a new land, a place my grandmother had described in stories.

"You really believe you'll find such a place?"

"I don't know." It hurt to say the words, to admit my doubt. "But I can't give up now."

"Are you sure?"

I nodded.

"Very well, then. I wish you luck." She reached behind her and produced two heavy sacks and dropped them to the ground. "Food for your journey. I hope you find what you're looking for—"

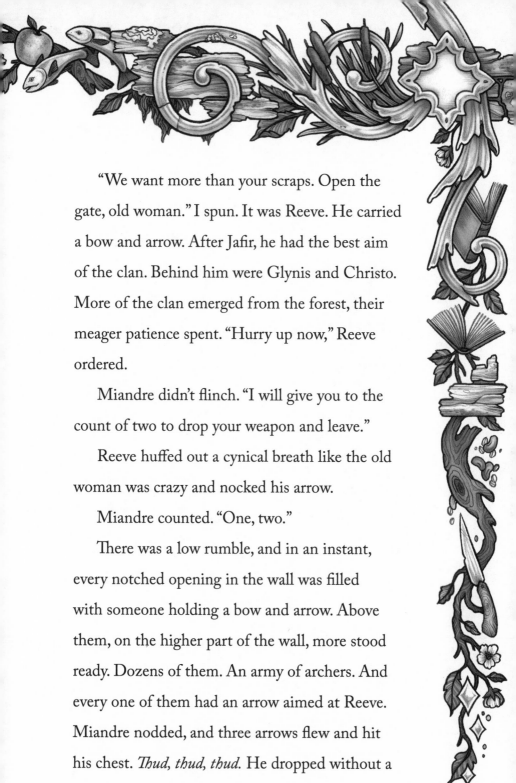

"We want more than your scraps. Open the gate, old woman." I spun. It was Reeve. He carried a bow and arrow. After Jafir, he had the best aim of the clan. Behind him were Glynis and Christo. More of the clan emerged from the forest, their meager patience spent. "Hurry up now," Reeve ordered.

Miandre didn't flinch. "I will give you to the count of two to drop your weapon and leave."

Reeve huffed out a cynical breath like the old woman was crazy and nocked his arrow.

Miandre counted. "One, two."

There was a low rumble, and in an instant, every notched opening in the wall was filled with someone holding a bow and arrow. Above them, on the higher part of the wall, more stood ready. Dozens of them. An army of archers. And every one of them had an arrow aimed at Reeve. Miandre nodded, and three arrows flew and hit his chest. *Thud, thud, thud.* He dropped without a

word or grunt. Dead. The clan froze, making no more advances. Disbelief hung in the air.

"I am a woman of my word," Miandre finally called out. "Which of you is the leader?"

Fergus walked forward and looked down at Reeve's still body. "You've made a big mistake, old woman."

"Your powers of observation are not too keen, are they?" Miandre replied. "It's quite obvious who has made the mistake. Now I will give the rest of you another count of two to gather the bags I've offered and head back to your camp. I expect you all to be out of this valley before nightfall."

She paused, locking eyes with Fergus, and then began counting. "One—"

Everyone scrambled. Glynis and Christo grabbed the food sacks. Fergus and Steffan grabbed me, and we were all running back into the woods for the horses, and then the trail.

I paid for my failure, but it was worth it.

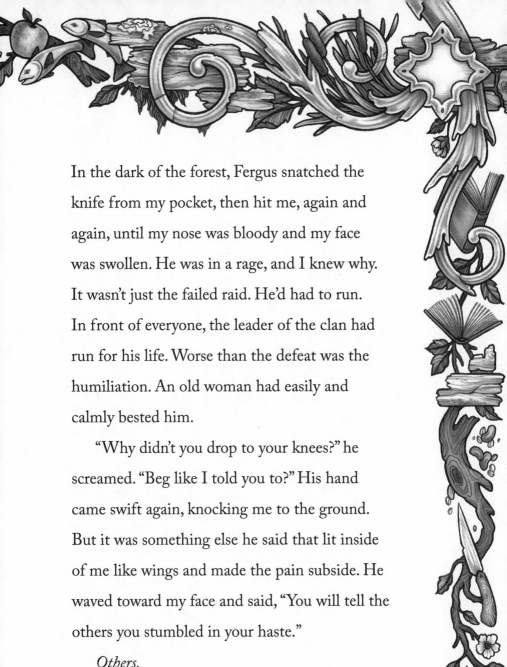

In the dark of the forest, Fergus snatched the
knife from my pocket, then hit me, again and
again, until my nose was bloody and my face
was swollen. He was in a rage, and I knew why.
It wasn't just the failed raid. He'd had to run.
In front of everyone, the leader of the clan had
run for his life. Worse than the defeat was the
humiliation. An old woman had easily and
calmly bested him.

"Why didn't you drop to your knees?" he
screamed. "Beg like I told you to?" His hand
came swift again, knocking me to the ground.
But it was something else he said that lit inside
of me like wings and made the pain subside. He
waved toward my face and said, "You will tell the
others you stumbled in your haste."

Others.

It wasn't Jafir alone who he wanted me to
lie to anymore. He wanted me to lie to the
others too.

CHAPTER TWENTY-SIX

MORRIGHAN

THE NEXT DAYS WERE RELENTLESS, BEYOND THE
pale of what we had already endured. It wasn't
the path we took, but Fergus. His humiliation at
Tor's Watch poured out onto all of us. His voice
became louder, his words demeaning and cruel.
No one was spared, including Laurida. He heaped
blame on her for collapsing before the raid. It was
her fault that everything went wrong. The pace he
made us keep was his punishment.

I begged him to slow down, saying Laurida
needed a few days' rest to regain her strength. She
rode Jafir's horse, but it wasn't enough, and one
day she fell from it, too weak to hold on. I wasn't

sure if it was her spirit that was failing, or her body. She died minutes later, right there on the trail. I dared a long condemning stare at Fergus. *She needed rest.* His only response was to order us to bury her. Jafir wept and whispered words against Laurida's forehead before he placed her in her grave. And then his hand went to his knife. Jonas, Christo, and two others of the clan went for theirs.

Not yet, I whispered, grabbing his arm. *We're too close.*

But were we? Was I lying to Jafir? I felt as lost as ever. Time and distance had become water slipping through my fingers, immeasurable, elusive. They had no meaning.

I didn't know where we were, or if this once-upon-a-time world of Ama's even existed anymore. My mind began to travel elsewhere in those grueling days, traveling across the miles, across time. I felt myself sitting in Ama's lap, a

child again, her strong arms around me. It all seemed so real. *Shhh, the scavengers are close.* She whispered stories in my ear to quiet me. *Once upon a time, my child, there was a princess no bigger than you. The world was at her fingertips. She commanded, and the light obeyed. The sun, moon, and stars knelt and rose at her touch. Once upon a time . . .*

I heard other voices as well. Venda's. Sometimes I thought I was losing my sanity, because I barely remembered my aunt, and yet her voice was clear, coming to me again and again. It didn't comfort me but was a weight in my gut instead. She would call my name and weep. She would speak of thieves, and dragons, and tears.

In those endless miles, I also thought about Miandre, how perceptive she was, how strong. How unwavering and sure of herself she was. *I know their ways.* Now I did too. I tried to think about her when doubts flooded in.

The days stretched on endlessly, and the

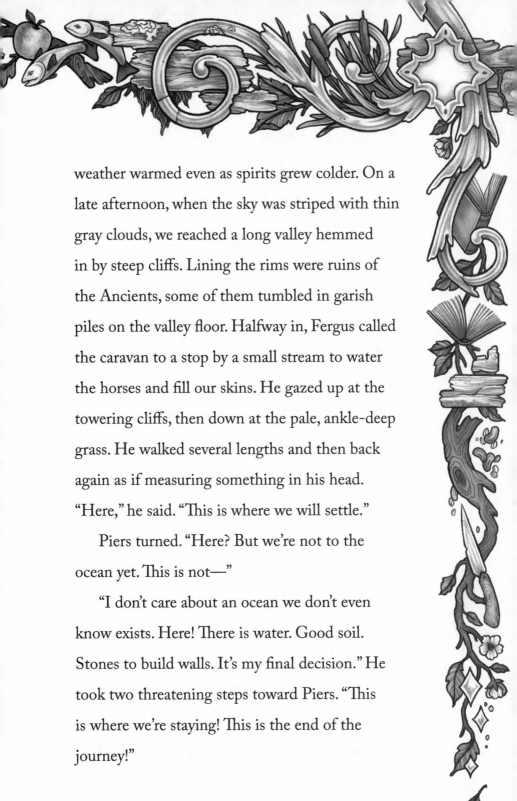

weather warmed even as spirits grew colder. On a
late afternoon, when the sky was striped with thin
gray clouds, we reached a long valley hemmed
in by steep cliffs. Lining the rims were ruins of
the Ancients, some of them tumbled in garish
piles on the valley floor. Halfway in, Fergus called
the caravan to a stop by a small stream to water
the horses and fill our skins. He gazed up at the
towering cliffs, then down at the pale, ankle-deep
grass. He walked several lengths and then back
again as if measuring something in his head.
"Here," he said. "This is where we will settle."

Piers turned. "Here? But we're not to the
ocean yet. This is not—"

"I don't care about an ocean we don't even
know exists. Here! There is water. Good soil.
Stones to build walls. It's my final decision." He
took two threatening steps toward Piers. "This
is where we're staying! This is the end of the
journey!"

But there was no fruit. No gardens. No apparent game. Only the rubble of the Ancients to build tall walls.

By then everyone in the clan had stopped what they were doing and turned. The silence was thick. Piers stared at him, slack-jawed.

But Fergus didn't stop there. His next words were ones I had expected all along once the journey ended. For him to give me what I had bargained for was the same as giving away power, and power was all that mattered to him, especially now that he had a new world in his grasp.

"And you," he said, pointing at me, "you have not pleased me as we bargained. You are to be Steffan's wife." He turned to Jafir and drew his knife. "Which means you will pay in flesh the debt you owe the clan for your betrayal."

His life. That was the debt Jafir owed. For showing compassion. For falling in love.

Steffan possessively jerked me toward him like

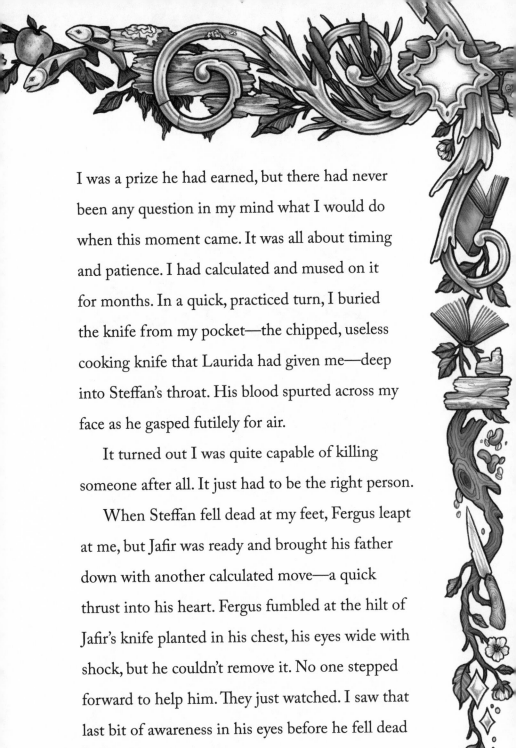

I was a prize he had earned, but there had never been any question in my mind what I would do when this moment came. It was all about timing and patience. I had calculated and mused on it for months. In a quick, practiced turn, I buried the knife from my pocket—the chipped, useless cooking knife that Laurida had given me—deep into Steffan's throat. His blood spurted across my face as he gasped futilely for air.

It turned out I was quite capable of killing someone after all. It just had to be the right person.

When Steffan fell dead at my feet, Fergus leapt at me, but Jafir was ready and brought his father down with another calculated move—a quick thrust into his heart. Fergus fumbled at the hilt of Jafir's knife planted in his chest, his eyes wide with shock, but he couldn't remove it. No one stepped forward to help him. They just watched. I saw that last bit of awareness in his eyes before he fell dead beside his son.

None mourned their loss. None reached for weapons to retaliate, and Piers declared Jafir the new head of the clan.

I was eighteen when we reached the true place of staying. A place where a summer moon, pink and swollen, sat low in a starry sky, and the sun rose warm and welcoming on our faces. A place where red fruit the size of fists hung from trees and a line of deep blue stretched across the horizon as far as we could see.

In the distance, a golden bridge, grander than anything I could imagine, rose from a sparkling bay. Thick green foliage ate up the remnants of ruins on hillsides, making them impossibly beautiful. Deer roamed in herds on hilltops, and birds of every color were plentiful in the air.

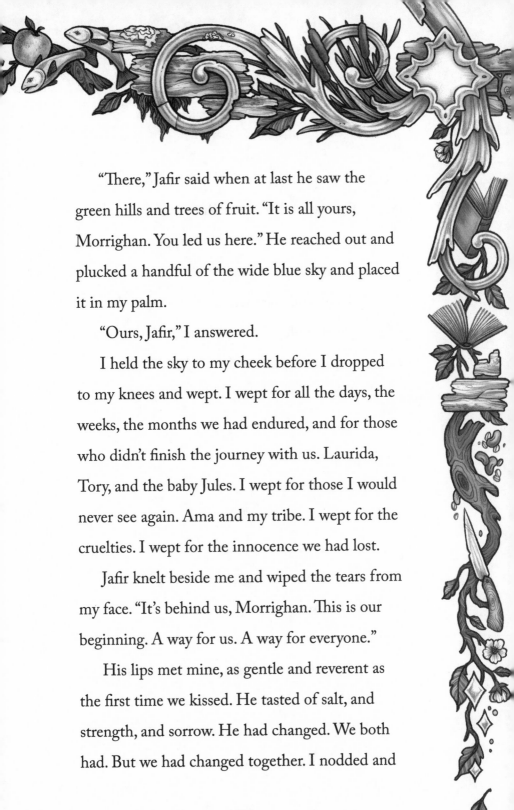

"There," Jafir said when at last he saw the green hills and trees of fruit. "It is all yours, Morrighan. You led us here." He reached out and plucked a handful of the wide blue sky and placed it in my palm.

"Ours, Jafir," I answered.

I held the sky to my cheek before I dropped to my knees and wept. I wept for all the days, the weeks, the months we had endured, and for those who didn't finish the journey with us. Laurida, Tory, and the baby Jules. I wept for those I would never see again. Ama and my tribe. I wept for the cruelties. I wept for the innocence we had lost.

Jafir knelt beside me and wiped the tears from my face. "It's behind us, Morrighan. This is our beginning. A way for us. A way for everyone."

His lips met mine, as gentle and reverent as the first time we kissed. He tasted of salt, and strength, and sorrow. He had changed. We both had. But we had changed together. I nodded and

our hands wove together and we prayed, to one god or four, we didn't know. But we gave thanks, praying that this was truly the end, praying it was the new beginning we had sought.

We stood and watched as the clan ran ahead of us into the valley that would become our home. I listened to their cries and their laughter and watched them swing in circles, dancing, their heads thrown back with joy.

The stories were true.

You were right, Ama, I whispered in my head. *Such a place exists.*

Jafir pulled me close, watching too, and he pressed his hand to the small mound growing in my belly and smiled.

Our hope.

"We've been blessed by your gods," he said. "The cruelties of the world are behind us now. Our child will never know them."

I closed my eyes, wanting to believe him.

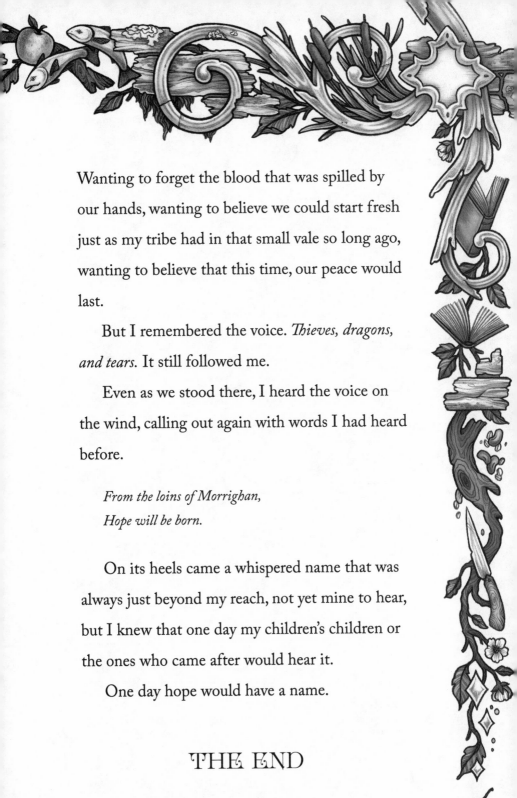

Wanting to forget the blood that was spilled by our hands, wanting to believe we could start fresh just as my tribe had in that small vale so long ago, wanting to believe that this time, our peace would last.

But I remembered the voice. *Thieves, dragons, and tears.* It still followed me.

Even as we stood there, I heard the voice on the wind, calling out again with words I had heard before.

From the loins of Morrighan,
Hope will be born.

On its heels came a whispered name that was always just beyond my reach, not yet mine to hear, but I knew that one day my children's children or the ones who came after would hear it.

One day hope would have a name.

THE END

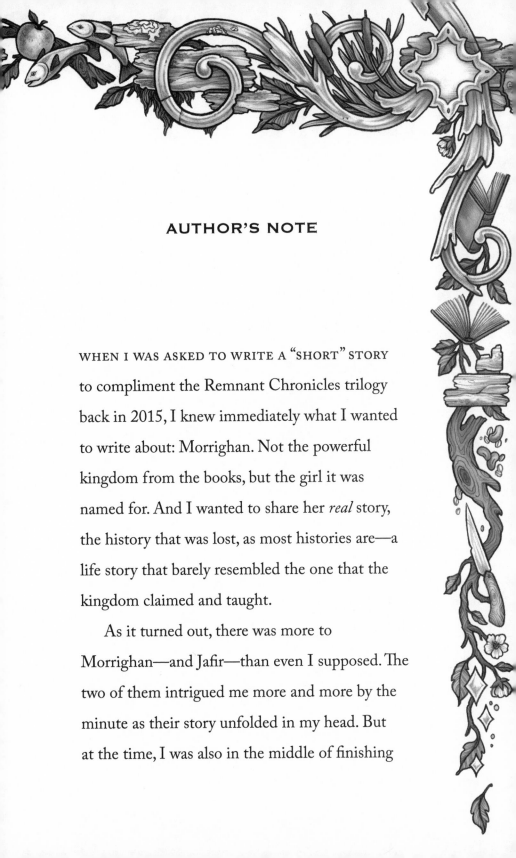

AUTHOR'S NOTE

WHEN I WAS ASKED TO WRITE A "SHORT" STORY to compliment the Remnant Chronicles trilogy back in 2015, I knew immediately what I wanted to write about: Morrighan. Not the powerful kingdom from the books, but the girl it was named for. And I wanted to share her *real* story, the history that was lost, as most histories are—a life story that barely resembled the one that the kingdom claimed and taught.

As it turned out, there was more to Morrighan—and Jafir—than even I supposed. The two of them intrigued me more and more by the minute as their story unfolded in my head. But at the time, I was also in the middle of finishing

up *The Beauty of Darkness*, the conclusion of the trilogy, with the duology spin-off—which was still to come—already lurking in the back of my mind. Still, I thought I had time to write just one "little" story. When my editor checked in with me and asked, *That short story almost done?* I answered, *Almost.* Several times. But the truth was, Morrighan's and Jafir's story had taken off in my head. I was captivated and couldn't let them go. The short story grew, by ten pages, twenty, sixty. Gulp. I finally had to wrap it up, but by then it had grown into a novella.

It was published as an ebook, but I always had a secret wish that one day it might be published as a hardcover book so it could be read and displayed along with the rest of the Remnant family. I heard from so many readers wishing the same. And then in the fall of 2021, my editor broached the idea of doing just that, publishing it as a special edition with art and bonus material if I was interested.

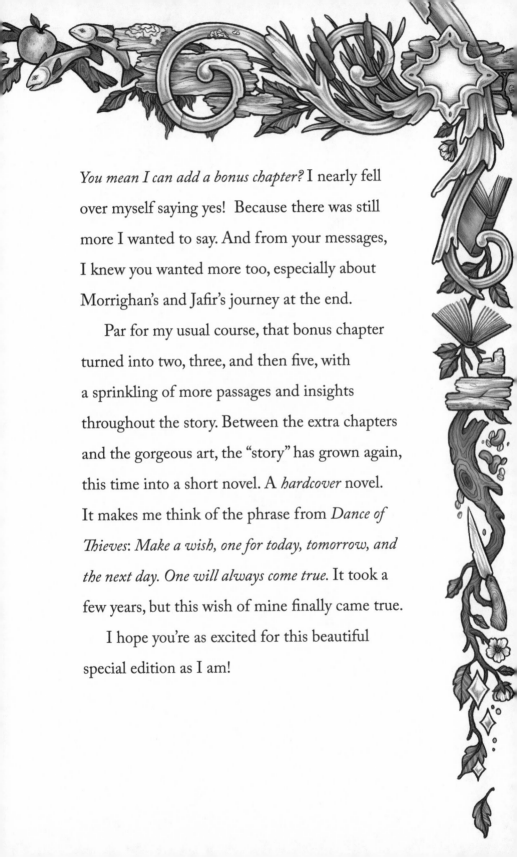

You mean I can add a bonus chapter? I nearly fell over myself saying yes! Because there was still more I wanted to say. And from your messages, I knew you wanted more too, especially about Morrighan's and Jafir's journey at the end.

Par for my usual course, that bonus chapter turned into two, three, and then five, with a sprinkling of more passages and insights throughout the story. Between the extra chapters and the gorgeous art, the "story" has grown again, this time into a short novel. A *hardcover* novel. It makes me think of the phrase from *Dance of Thieves*: *Make a wish, one for today, tomorrow, and the next day. One will always come true.* It took a few years, but this wish of mine finally came true.

I hope you're as excited for this beautiful special edition as I am!

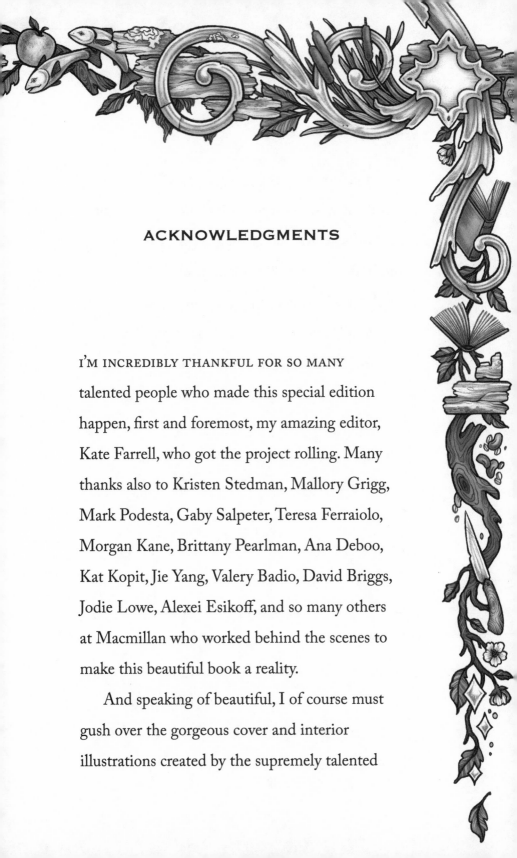

ACKNOWLEDGMENTS

I'M INCREDIBLY THANKFUL FOR SO MANY talented people who made this special edition happen, first and foremost, my amazing editor, Kate Farrell, who got the project rolling. Many thanks also to Kristen Stedman, Mallory Grigg, Mark Podesta, Gaby Salpeter, Teresa Ferraiolo, Morgan Kane, Brittany Pearlman, Ana Deboo, Kat Kopit, Jie Yang, Valery Badio, David Briggs, Jodie Lowe, Alexei Esikoff, and so many others at Macmillan who worked behind the scenes to make this beautiful book a reality.

And speaking of beautiful, I of course must gush over the gorgeous cover and interior illustrations created by the supremely talented

Kate O'Hara. That cover is seriously frameable and I love how her interior illustrations brought the joys, sorrows, and challenges of Morrighan's and Jafir's world to life. Thank you.

A huge bouquet of thanks to my agent, Rosemary Stimola, and her stellar team. They are the best and I'm so grateful to them for bringing this story to readers all over the world.

Thank you to my fellow writers who offered advice, encouragement, perspective, or a good laugh when I needed it: Marlene Perez, Melissa Wyatt, Alyson Noël, Jill Rubalcaba, Tricia Levenseller, Brigid Kemmerer, and Stephanie Garber. And thanks to on-the-spot readers Jessica and Karen, who offered immediate feedback and insights.

Always and forever, love and gratitude for my family, my rock and joy. You keep life magical.

And huge weepy thanks to you, the readers. Ultimately, you made this happen. Your support,

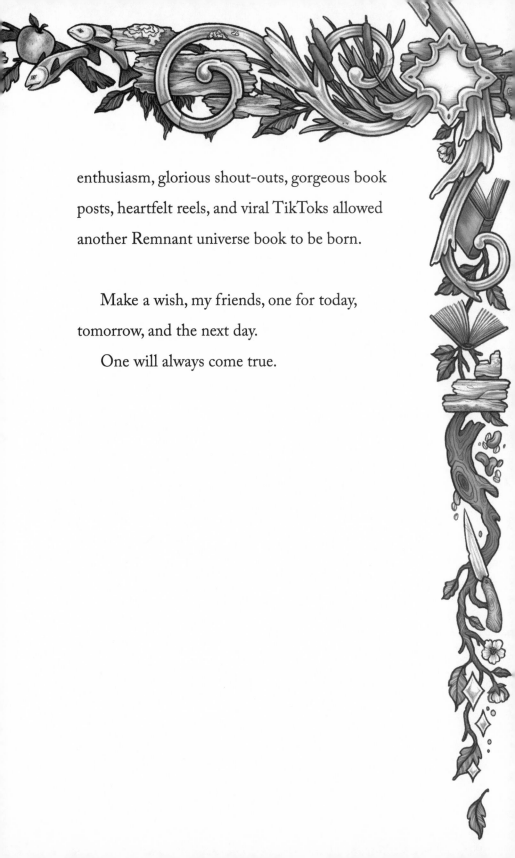

enthusiasm, glorious shout-outs, gorgeous book posts, heartfelt reels, and viral TikToks allowed another Remnant universe book to be born.

Make a wish, my friends, one for today, tomorrow, and the next day.

One will always come true.

DISCOVER THE REST
OF THE BESTSELLING
REMNANT UNIVERSE

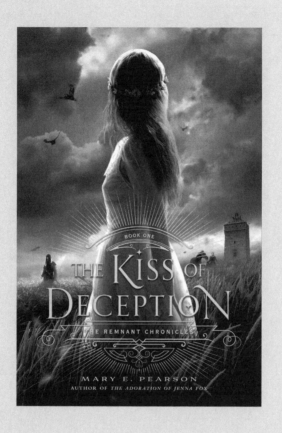

★ "Pearson offers readers a wonderfully full-bodied story: harrowing, romantic, and full of myth and memory, fate and hope ... This has the sweep of an epic tale, told with some twists." —**BOOKLIST**, starred review

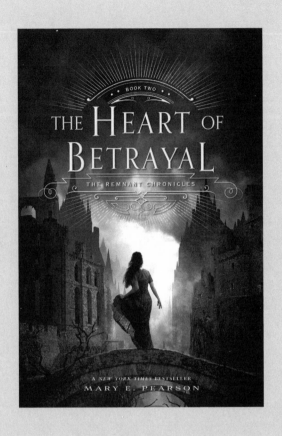

★ "It's rare that the second book in a
series is as good—or perhaps better—
than the first, but that's the case here."
—*BOOKLIST*, starred review

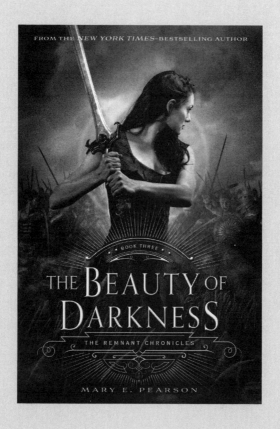

"Readers will be gripping pages from
the nerve-wracking start through the heart-
stopping ending . . . Pearson's Remnant
Chronicles is an epic YA series to get behind."
—ROMANTIC TIMES

"This action-filled novel, set in a high fantasy
world, has it all: romance, adventure, mysticism,
and heroism."—SCHOOL LIBRARY JOURNAL

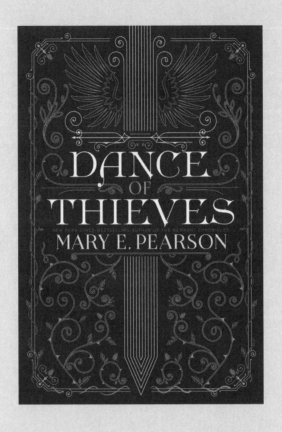

"Pearson is a gifted storyteller ... Fans will
thrill at these newest protagonists, especially the
women warriors." —**PUBLISHERS WEEKLY**

"Slow-burning, seductive romance, layers of twists,
and action-packed adventure." —**BOOKLIST**

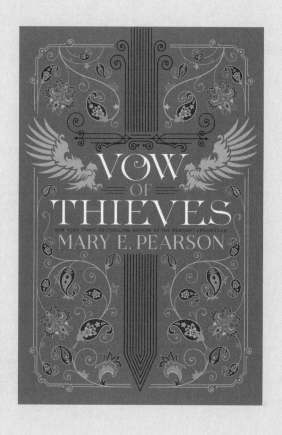

★ "Kazi and Jase find themselves facing down
an enemy they never saw coming. A breathtaking
sequel." —**BOOKLIST**, starred review

"A smashing, satisfying adventure!" —**KIRKUS**